The Allotment Gang

By

Steven Carter

Grosvenor House
Publishing Limited

This book is published by
Grosvenor House Publishing Ltd
Link House
140 The Broadway, Tolworth, Surrey, KT6 7HT.
www.grosvenorhousepublishing.co.uk

This book is a work of fiction. Any resemblance to
people or events, past or present, is purely coincidental.

A CIP record for this book
is available from the British Library

Paperback ISBN 978-1-83615-541-6

For Nell

Notes and acknowledgements:

Steven and I have been friends since our School days in Bromsgrove, our families close, our life memories shared. When he died, tragically too early, in 2022, his family asked me take on the responsibility for publishing this novel, which we do now in his memory, with the deepest effection for a life well led and a dearly missed friend.

While this book is notionally set in a world that is the North Worcestershire of our youth, at some point in the 1980's, at least before the internet, there are inconsistencies. Having edited the book several times, I have drawn the conclusion that the many non-time neutral references; to CCTV and the Onedin Line being on TV on a Saturday night, for example, do not matter at all. Neither do the geographical anomalies which might grate with those that know the landscape around Bromsgrove well. What matters in the honesty of Steven's approach to life, his search for an underlying philosophy, and his belief in the force of 'goodness' winning out in the end. All of this ethos, I believe, shines through.

The narrator of this book, Peter, does not have a final diary entry. Steven was a great diarist, so this surprises me. I did consider adding some final words from Peter, but have elected not to at this time. Steven will have had a reason for this omission.

My thanks to various people who have read and helped me edit this work in the last few years. A labour of love.

Written in the Southwold Sailors Reading Room, Southwold, Suffolk, on a bleak winters day in January 2025. Steven would have <u>loved</u> this place.

Final edits completed at Painters Forstal Community Hall, Nr Faversham, Kent. 16 June 2025

Professor Chris 'Ben' Bennett. Bay House, Painters Forstal, Kent.

Artwork by Rosie Philpott www.rosiephilpott.co.uk

Let not light see my black and deep desires.

Macbeth

Chapter One

It was late summer and the Star Inn allotments were verdant and filled with the soft sound of insects busying themselves before evening fell. The sunlight weighed the air down heavily and sent angular shapes of shadow and light across the fields. The air, thickened by the sunlight, was filled with pollen and dust that made it sweet smelling. Bees, corpulent with summer pollen and dressed in black and yellow coats, buzzed in circles around the plants. All around sat a great bounty in various shades and colours. From pinks and purples through yellows and oranges to every variant of nature's greens. Summer, often wet months, had seen unprecedented growth. Plants of all descriptions, sizes, smells and colours had pushed through the loamy earth and grown with such vigour and abundance that there seemed no end to nature's fulfilment. If you were of a wistful disposition, had the time to pause from your busy life and could watch carefully, you could practically see and hear the plants growing, straining against soil and air to produce life. The soil itself smelled of abundance, of fertility and of fecundity. Flowers bobbed in a myriad of colour and perfume. This small patch, forever England in its summer glory, was an Eden of sorts. There were no forbidden fruits here for this was a place of unlimited bounty and harvest. The work of man in collusion with nature. Harnessing the fruits of the soil. Beans, peas, lettuces, potato, tomatoes, carrots, sweet corn, marrows. All provender, bounty and beauty.

The allotments were all uniform rectangles, with grass and brick pathways separating one from another and making up a small field of work and pleasure. On one side of the allotment

1

ground was the old ruined Star Inn with its tiny car park. The sign for the Inn was long gone and the windows were bricked up and whitewashed. There was an outline in yellow and black of the Ansells brewery sign. The brewery in Aston was still functioning next to the HP sauce factory, but this old pub had passed its best. There were wires running parallel to each other along the pub walls and several trellises of wisteria, grapes and tomatoes grew up the brick work. The red tiles on the roof dipped in the middle like a well-worn sofa. The only functioning part of the Old Star Inn was the outhouse which still served as a toilet block for the Allotment. This little brick built flat roofed building had a two-man urinal, a stall, and two wash basins. The interior walls were freshly painted and the window sills contained a range of plants and seed trays. On one wall was a collection of old railway signs and on another a large star had been painted by a group of children a few years before.

A wall ran down the adjacent side of the allotment field and woods and farmers' fields were on the other two sides making the land feel enclosed and private, but still fully exposed to the summer sun. Each allotment had its own shed. Some were professionally made and expensive looking while others were hand built using flotsam and tin sheets painted all manner of colours. In places it looked like an upmarket refugee camp. The most interesting shed was made from corrugated iron which drummed when the rain fell. It was painted red green and gold and from one corner there was a flag pole flying the flag of Jamaica. There was a large green marijuana leaf painted on the door with a sign saying One Love in pink letters. A small chimney came out on one side made of drain pipe and cans. Next to the door hung a coat and a tea cosy hat in red gold and green. This shed sat at the edge of the far allotment next to the white washed wall of the old pub. It was organised and neat. Bamboo canes created structures that held up all manner of growth. In the dwindling summer sun there were squashes, chillies, and beans growing. A barrel of water with a wooden lid sat next to three compost bins made from wood. An old man bent over with a hoe that pushed the weeds away between the bamboo canes. He hummed as he worked.

At the centre of the allotment were three sheds, linked together with a central pergola. Vines hung down from it giving it a Mediterranean garden feel. Four elderly men sat round the table. Two were playing chess, one was smoking a pipe and reading the newspaper and the last one was looking out across the allotments with a look of pure contentment on his face. The look was so intensely content that it would have made the Buddha smile. They were all silent as only people happy in each other's company can be silent. The three sheds connected here were all made from good quality wood and had the appearance of being professionally constructed as if by a carpenter of some skill. They had windows and two of them had greenhouses attached on one side and one had boxes running the length of the shed with glass tops. There was not a window that was not cracked or broken in some way. However there seemed no urgency from the four men to put this right or to get up and till in the allotments. It was a scene of serenity, peace and relaxation. The allotments that circled the sheds here all were filled with the summer growth. Neat lines of potatoes, broad beans, carrots, onions and lettuces stretched across each space. Strawberries grew in terracotta pots and tomatoes in bags. Trellises of sweet pea flowers mingled with peas and a line of sunflowers nodded gracefully in the light breeze. All the food a person would need to sustain themselves grew here. But there were also flowers too, and bushes of blackberries and several of damson and plum trees. At the side of the farmland there was an allotment taken up with an apple and pear orchard of eight trees.

Most of the vegetable beds were raised and had old railway sleepers for sides. Some had cloches sitting in them and some were covered in fine green netting. Tayberries and Blackberries could be seen through the netting. The crops of vegetables were planted in neat lines within the borders of the raised beds. There was a strong smell of soil and compost. Sweetcorn grew like a forest dell in one section while salad crops dominated the sunny ground.

Allotments are all measured in rods, an Anglo-Saxon farming measure of about 5 metres. Ten rods are a full allotment, considered sufficient to feed a family for a year, and five rods being a half size. Most of the horticulturalists had five rod plots, but there were a number of ten rod plots. Surrounding the central shed area there were four full size allotments. The most extraordinary one ran from the central sheds to the woodland at the edge of the field. This allotment was split into two, with the shaded area nearer the woods given over to vegetables like rhubarb and various bushes of fruits such as redcurrant, gooseberries, blackberries and raspberries. A thin green net like a bride's veil hid them from the future passions of the birds. Away from the trees newly sown winter crops for harvesting later in the year like kale, spring cabbages, and spinach bore up and down the dirt in lines of little sprouting greenery. But it was the section of five rods nearest the sheds that bore the chaotic nature of a wild gardener without any sense of structure, that drew the eye. Whole sections of herbs fragranced the air. Angelica, chives, marjoram, rosemary, mint, sage, lemon balm, tarragon, thyme and parsley. It was as if a herbalist, a witch or a shaman, had constructed a slab of herbage ready for the pestle and mortar to make potions for the ill and infirm. Here there was a constellation of perfumes, made more vivid or subtle with the passing of a hand across the leaves and flowers. It was designed for touch and smell, for the gardener. Peter was a blind man. Peter now in his 70s had not always been blind, he had suffered with Retinitis Pigmentosa a disease of the eye which gradually and with great cruelty took away his vision in increments, until he could no longer see. There was light and dark in his visual world but little else.

Between the herbs and the fruits sat a traditional English cottage garden, more anarchic in its planting. The colours did not merge subtly like a good garden should, nor did the heights of the flowers have any consideration for form or structure. There were no rules except for the rules of smell and texture. Here in glorious technicolour was a flower arrangement so unique that no prize would ever be gifted except the prize of love. Hollyhocks with star shaped hairs and lobed, leaves whose flowers arranged in fascicles with notched petals of yellow, pink and white swayed dreamily in the balmy summer air. Amongst them Foxgloves with tall spiked and tubular flowers. Catmint with blue flowers and grey green foliage fought for the sunshine with Delphiniums at least 90 cm high. Surrounding the winding brick path, a single brick wide, grew peonies looking like ice-cream, geraniums and the large domed headed phlox. This was a place not of colour and light although there was plenty of it. This was an allotment of texture, smell and taste.

Peter was rarely seen at the garden. He came at night time during the weekend, being dropped off by his sister on her way to Friday night bingo, Saturday night Tango dancing and Sunday night Bridge Club. He always managed to get four hours of work in while the rest of the nation and allotment owners were in the pub or watching Dad's Army or the Onedin Line. His tired journey home to a small alms house cottage behind the church was filled with the gossip of the parish, a small bottled gift from bingo winnings or heavy sighs as Dorothy thought about the missed opportunity to tango with Roger, the local lothario and ex British tango champion from 1949.

Peter had been a teacher of philosophy until he lost his sight. He had decided to take ill health retirement rather than carry on teaching, although the local authority would have put in place measures to allow him to carry on. He had lost a little faith in his subject and more so in the quality of the students he had to deal with. Peter had a romantic view on philosophy, believing that it could both change the individual and the world. The early philosophers, he would often argue, gave advice in the same way that modern self-help books gave advice on how to live your life. But he felt that philosophy had wandered down too many cul de sacs and had lost its mojo as a means to change the world and becoming little more than intellectual masturbation. Philosophy had created communism and fascism and the net result of these dogmas was a herd response towards conflict and hatred and distress. People's lives had not been improved, satisfaction had not been gained and happiness was as elusive in the modern consumer world as it had been a century before. Peter's loss of faith in philosophy coincided with his loss of appetite to teach something he did not believe in to the next generation, and so he had left teaching and retired to the garden project. He often said that we needed to hold our beliefs and our thoughts lightly. And that was his final word on any philosophical argument that he engaged in. Peter missed reading most of all, especially the American literature of the 20s and 30s like Steinbeck, Fitzgerald,

Dos Pasos and Hemingway. Peter had yet to learn braille. He wrote a diary each day in neat copperplate handwriting, but he could not read any of the words back. Why he continued to write a diary was often beyond him. Force of habit was all he could think of or the tyranny of the empty page reflecting an equally empty life.

Peter had only one love in his life and she was married to one of his colleagues. He had spent years of faculty dinner parties always choosing to sit next to her, to talk and to bask in her smile. After a house party while her husband was away on a conference, they had both had too much to drink and he had walked her home and got into her bed. They had kissed passionately all night but she had resisted any further pressure of love making, telling him that she could not afford to fall any more in love with him than she already was. A year later she had moved with her husband to Lancaster and he had not seen or heard from her since. Perhaps she thought that the kissing was a greater betrayal, but to Peter the loneliness that had always been a part of his life now consumed it.

The smallest plot and yet the most productive in the field was in the possession of the local vicar. One Reverend James Smith MBE, PhD (Oxon). The Reverend rarely attended to his plot, only occasionally turning up on an old Vespa scooter to harvest the crop which had miraculously grown in the most sumptuous and verdant manner. What the allotment was used for was creating food for the poor of the parish. Fresh vegetables were always a part of all the food deliveries to the elderly or unemployed families within ten miles of the church. The Reverend was aware that the abundance generated from his allotment was disproportionate to its size and his efforts. But he turned a blind eye to the miracle of plot six only occasionally leaving a bottle of whiskey or rum on the communal garden table as gratitude to nature's abundance and the hard work of the Allotment Gang as he referred to the men and women who toiled there. Needless to observe that the food bounty was fulsome and regular, if not on occasion lifesaving, and always life affirming. His harvest festival service and sermon always contained the notion of dressing the land with abundance and recreating an Eden of sorts. Of clothing the workers of the land in virtue, kindness and compassion. The sermon brought a smile to everyone's face because everyone knew it was the right way to live life and it was the right thing to do. The Reverend would stand and discuss the miracles of nature and of God's hand in this life knowing that he had several bottles of wine in the vestry and a year of prayer for the souls of the men and women of this little part of England's soil. So, on this small holy patch grew potatoes, carrots, cabbages and beans and peas of various varieties. But the harvested plot delivered all manner of fruits, squashes, kale, marrows, sweet corn and occasional pots of honey none of which could be observed growing in the vicar's patch.

The smartest and neatest of the allotments was run by Hans Schmitt, an Austrian anglophile, who true to his age, nationality and stereotyping enjoyed order, tidiness and straight lines. His shed was freshly painted every year and no object remained broken, squeaky or untied. Nature was ordered and controlled and would remain so on his watch. Hans was tall and thin and looked in his old age like an ex professional footballer. He was a man who looked after himself, ate and drank frugally and kept an almost Aristotelian sense of calm across his humours. His angular face and strong blue eyes made him a vision of Teutonic wellbeing. Hans spoke softly and with more than a hint of accent despite being fluent in English and having lived in rural

Worcestershire since 1944. Like many big men he was of a gentle disposition and had a liking for dogs and cats. His dog, a little terrier, was called Monty after the British Field Marshall. The dog doted on him and would follow him around the allotment lying down on the soil twitching an ear against an irritating fly while Hans was working. Hans was the chess player sat opposite Tom, who he played most evenings after work, particularly in the summer months when the light warm evenings were rarely interrupted by rain.

Peter's diary

It is always wonderful to be in the garden in the early evening in summer. The noise of the bees and the birds is especially wonderful. I can hear them around me, I am surrounded in song and the industrious activity of Freddie's bees. When I could see I barely listened and would block out most sounds from my conscious world. Now I can no longer see I am immersed in a cacophony of music. My head spins at times because I do not know where the sounds are all coming from but then as I sit or work quietly, I can relax into the din and then the din becomes broken down into its component parts. I have learned the sounds of the different birds using a tape machine in the library and a cassette that Marianne, the librarian, has found for me called great British bird song. The narrator says which bird is singing and if I don't know the bird by shape and colour in my mind's eye then Marianne will find a picture in the book shelves and describe to me what they look like. I can visualise thirty garden birds now just from the song or the hawking rasping sounds of crows to the delightful orchestra of sound that a black bird will sing. Marianne found me the first ever recording on BBC radio of people singing with Nightingales. Though I have yet to hear one here in the allotments. Tonight, it has been a humid and warm way into the late evening. Often, I am alone at this time. The new man is here on weekends but I never hear him working. There are noises from his shed where he seems to entertain a different woman because I can smell different perfumes each Friday as they crunch along his gravelled path. Everywhere else the paths are bricks and act to demarcate the allotments. I have planted a short hedge of lavender at the end of my patch between myself and the middle sheds. I grew all the plants from seed and set them in the ground today. They already have long strands of flowers. My hands and sleeves smell of lavender. I could hear muttering going on in the area of the sheds as I worked. Greggory was smoking in his shed and Reverend James was standing quietly among his plants. I knew it was him from the sound of his steps and the fact that he just stands and takes it all in. Sometimes he will call out to me but mostly he just stands there, occasionally filling his nostrils with the smell of green and yellow. I know he likes the smell of green and yellow. I hope it is green and yellow for that is the smell I have allocated to the colours.

Chapter Two

The morning after a wet and humid summer night, Tom was at the bedroom window of his small maisonette watching. He stood with his hands on the curtains, just to one side of the window next to the old campaign chest where he kept his wife's clothes still. In the background the radio news was talking with the Prime Minister. She sounded tired, he thought as she often did when being interviewed by journalists that she had little regard for. Her voice had changed since being elected; it was slightly lower now than it had been. She spoke slowly as if to a naughty child. The journalist kept interrupting her with "But Mrs Thatcher" or "But Prime Minister". She ignored all the interjections and continued with her plodding dialogue on how Britain would work its way out of recession and that the media should stop finding fault when there was none. Tom was small for his generation and a little stooped across the shoulders. His face was thin and angular and his eyes were sunken into the sockets making his face part skeleton part flesh. His eyes were grey and piercing when he was angry and warm and convincing when he was relaxed. They looked like they had spent a lifetime weeping and were watery and heavy lidded. Tom wore a shirt buttoned to the neck but no tie, an old green cardigan with grey flannel trousers ending in tartan socks and brown slip-on slippers. His hair was thin and slicked back, moist against his head with Pomade which made him look like he had just stepped in from the rain. At 75 he was an old man, but hid his age well behind a clear and nimble mind and strong physique. He retained a wiry muscularity partly because he still did a weekly yoga class and worked hard in the allotments. Age was just a number to Tom and he lived his life in defiance of the aging process even when it seemed like a never-ending losing battle. He ate well, read a lot, kept the sedentary lifestyle at bay by avoiding television and keeping busy with various hobbies and interests.

Tom was not a nosey neighbour, not usually a twitcher of curtains, and was slightly embarrassed to be the voyeur of the morning scene next door. But he had been drawn to the window by the noise outside of the milkman and the young woman in the house next door arguing. Or rather, he was arguing and she was pleading. She was wrapped in a shawl over a night shirt which showed her thin white legs. In her arms was a baby sucking on a dummy. The woman was crying. It was not a scene he wished to remember.

"You have to pay me dear or there will be no milk," said the milkman.

"I am trying, but I can't cope with the benefits and I am struggling to get a job, what with the cost of child care and everything." the woman pleaded.

"Look I have given you three chances to pay up. I can't carry on like this. I am not a charity. I have my own family to consider. People aren't using milkmen any more now they can get their milk from the supermarkets. In ten years, we will not exist as a profession. I am struggling myself to make ends meet."

The milkman was dressed in a traditional white coat to his knees with beige trousers and understandably comfortable shoes.

"Please. I need it for the baby." she said.

And so, it went. The milk undelivered and a child in need. It broke Tom's heart to see such a thing. He quickly changed out of his pyjamas pulled on a satchel filled with leaflets and left the house. After a chat with the milkman at the end of his road, Tom started delivering his leaflets. As he went up and down the garden paths a group of small children started to follow him.

"What are you doing Mr?" came the question from a small boy in blue shorts and a t- shirt.

"I'm delivering leaflets to all these houses," said Tom

"Leaflets about what?"

"Leaflets explaining how they can have a better life," replied Tom mysteriously. He held the leaflets dramatically against his chest to hide the contents, as if they were a deep secret.

"Like winning the pools?" said a little blonde boy in corduroy trousers and batman t-shirt.

"Exactly like winning the pools son," replied Tom.

"Can we help Mr?"

"Sorry son this is too big a job for you little ones." Tom winked. "Maybe when you are a bit more grown up."

"Oh, go on Mr."

After the crowd of small children pleaded as one, Tom said it was alright and he started to dish out a leaflet to each child as he walked up the road. Within a few minutes he had seven children helping and marching next to him keeping step as he whistled the tune from The Great Escape. His leaflet round which normally took him two hours was finished in thirty minutes. The children returned to kicking a can against the curb stone and filled with the late summer boredom that comes at the end of the long school holidays.

Later that day Tom and Hans sat facing each other over a chess board at the allotment. Hans was rolling a cigarette and Tom was smoking a pipe. They wore well-worn jackets with patches on the elbows and thick red checked shirts and ragged corduroy trousers. Both wore wellington boots turned over at the calf. Hans wore a flat cap over his bald head and Tom had on a straw fedora.

"I watched her Hans," Tom said "and there was nothing I could really do. A single mother alone and broke with a small child and she could not even afford the milk. Terry is a good man but I could hear him saying he had a family to feed as well and he could not keep giving her free milk. It's just like the 1930s again. The poverty and the hopelessness that many suffer is the same. We may be wearing better clothes and our homes are less squalid but I'd hoped we had moved on. All I see on the television are rich people, beautiful people, happy people, but the reality is very different."

"So, what did you do?" said Hans.

"I walked down the road and caught Terry up and asked him how much she owed and when he told me, I gave him £10. I couldn't afford it myself but I could not see the child go hungry, not in the 1980s, not in one of the richest countries in the world. He went back to the house and left some milk for her.'

"You're a good man Thomas." Hans smiled, as Thomas winced at the words.

"There's no point being a good man anymore. The country wants wheelers and dealers and spivs and crooks for leaders. It doesn't want people like us. They are closing down the factories and the mines. It's all service industry now rather than manufacturing. Get rich quick and the wealth will trickle down to us plebs, so they say. But we will not see it. The days of the factory floor and a job for life are behind us. The dole queues are growing. I'd hate to be young again now."

"We didn't have it that good Tom. I think you are forgetting a small matter of trying to kill one another for six years. There was a lot of unpleasantness back then and it was a lot tougher. I prefer to live now in peace. Life is not about being happy all the time, it's about being content, that's far more important to me now. As I got older, I felt the weight of expectation about life lifting off my shoulders. That's why I come here. I'm content here. I like the physical work and I like the company. Living life by the rhythms of the seasons and the day light and night time is a good way to feel alive."

"I feel the same. This place is my escape."

"What is she called?" said Hans.

"Who?" said Tom.

"The girl."

"She's called Jennifer. She is very pretty. Beautiful pellucid eyes."

"Does she know you paid the bill?"

"I told Terry not to tell her. Just to say he'd had second thoughts, that's all. Valorie would never have forgiven me if I had not stepped in. She'd have been down the stairs like a shot and given Terry an earful and made him give her the milk. She was like that. She stood up for everyone. It did get her into a little trouble. She tried to slap our Member of Parliament once. She had fire in her that lady."

"Did you go and see her today?" said Hans.

"No, not today. The silly old man talking to a gravestone."

"It's not silly Thomas."

"I took her some Sweet Peas yesterday. They were always her favourite, delicate and yet sturdy, just like she was."

"What do you say to her?" said Hans.

"Oh, I don't know. Tell her about what's going on in the world, not much good news there. If there is any news from the children. Tell her I love her and miss her, when I am feeling particularly sad."

"In times like this I like to think of the first law of thermodynamics." said Hans

"What's that?"

"It states that the Universe is a closed system so no energy can be created or destroyed. So therefore, when you die not a bit of you is gone, you are just less orderly. The collection of atoms that made you are simply repurposed. So, the essence of you will continue to bless the Universe until the end of time."

"Nice idea."

"Were there any other women before her? Or were you childhood sweethearts?" asked Hans.

"There were other women before her. Several in fact. They all went the same way. First, they like you, then they will do anything for you and love you truly and deeply. Then with me they became bored until someone more interesting, more exciting or better looking came along. Then they leave filled with recrimination. Valorie was never like that. We started as we ended. Better than happy, as you say contented. There were never arguments even when I behaved like an arse. Each day swirled in a soup of contentment and this brought happiness and children. And now she has gone."

"I will tell her tomorrow about Jenny and how I was the Knight in shining armour who paid for the milk. What I'd like to do is go and get some of the money these rich people have and give it to the likes of Jenny."

"Not so much a knight in shining armour, more like Robbin Hood." said Hans, laughing.

"There's a lot of merit in that old legend. Did you have the same story in Germany?"

"Yes of course there are no new stories really, Johannes Buckler, Schinderhannes. It did not turn out well for him.

He and his outlaw band went to the guillotine when Germany was under Napoleonic rule. I'm sure he deserved it, certainly he was lucky to be remembered fondly for being a thief and a brute. Not like your Robin Hood."

"I've never stolen anything in my life. Have you?"

"Yes, during the war we took what we wanted; it didn't seem like theft. Mostly food and wine. When I was captured by the British, I had six good watches in my possession. They did not like that at all and I was given a beating before being handed over to the intelligence people without a watch to my name. Before the war started, as part of our paratrooper training, we would plan to rob banks and had to provide these plans to our training team to assess how viable they were. It's funny to remember that after all these years.'

"Did you pass?" said Tom.

"Of course, I passed. I was in the elite of the army. A proper soldier not like the Nazis brownshirt thugs."

The sound of a scratchy recording of Billie Holiday singing broke the conversation. The men listened as Freddie and Greggory arrived to join them, both walking stiffly after an afternoon of toiling.

> I don't know why but I'm feeling so sad
> I long to try something I never had
> Never had no kissin'
> Oh, what I've been missin'
> Lover man, oh, where can you be?
> The night is cold and I'm so all alone
> I'd give my soul just to call you my own
> Got a moon above me
> But no one to love me
> Lover man, oh, where can you be?

Freddie was tall and ramrod straight like a guardsman and very good looking. Some said Hollywood handsome. He was slim with wide shoulders like a swimmer and dressed smartly for the labouring he had been doing that day. His shirt was open at the neck and he wore a gold and red cravat. He was the very model of a dapper English gentleman. Freddie was one of those people who seems to avoid misfortune at every opportunity. He passed through life on a cloud of contentment. He knew he had been lucky in life. He believed that misfortune like happiness attaches itself to people like a curse. Some people are just unlucky in life and some are blessed. It was rarely a result of character, education or attitude, it was all to do with fortune and fate. While some people staggered from one crisis to another Freddie traversed life's obstacles with a benign serenity. He had found that he went through life feeling content with most of his desires realised without the nature of the world getting in his way. In fact, Freddie believed sincerely that misfortune had befallen the people who had got in his way or had treated him badly. It was like he had some kind of protective spirit that not only looked after him, but also punished the people who sought to do him ill. It was if the spirit could see that Freddie was a good decent man who needed protection from the injustices of life. Freddie had noticed it all his life, firstly at school where bullies often met unpleasant ends and even during the war, the pilots around him who mocked his good looks and dress sense often ended up charred in the English Channel. Call it karma, call it good luck, but Freddie was always surrounded by this and his personality, which was kind and generous, shone from him.

Greggory was diminutive and slender, his waist no more than 28 inches even at his age. He was black and had dreadlocks which grew out of a large woollen hat of green, red and yellow. He had a goatee beard which was pointed at the end and he wore dark rimmed NHS spectacles. They sat down at one end of the table as smoke from Tom's pipe swirled around them and up into the hanging vines. They sat listening to the song and Greggory rubbed his shoulders with something out of a tube then sipped loudly from a metal mug. Freddie flipped open a newspaper and began to read over half-moon spectacles.

"What are you old fellas talking about?" said Greggory grinning at the table of old men, of which he was the oldest by a good few years.

"Robbing banks," said Hans. Freddie looked up from his newspaper.

"We are talking about the perfect criminal and that is one that no one in their right mind would even consider suspecting. A gang perhaps of the same sort of person, no one would suspect a gang of old blokes who are as respectable as they come, church going, god fearing, war heroes and pillars of the local community."

"And why would they want to rob a bank after years being goodly men?" said Freddie.

Tom replied: "There is a lot of injustice in the modern world. The have-nots have never had it so bad. I was thinking about doing a bank and giving the money away."

Tom looked up from the chess board and smiled at his friends.

"Robin Hood?" said Freddie.

"Yes, a bit more like Robbing Tom," said Hans, winking at Tom.

"Well count me in," said Freddie half-heartedly. "I could do with a little excitement in my life." He yawned and stretched his arms and the newspaper above his head.

"Are you lot being serious?" asked Greggory, "or have you been on the damson wine?"

"Now there's a thought," said Freddie, getting up and walking into his shed. A few moments later he reappeared with two bottles and four tin mugs.

"The nettle wine is my favourite. It may already be the last one. Was saving it to accompany a ridiculous conversation and we are certainly in the realms of nettle wine this fine evening." Freddie tapped the two bottles with his fist full of mugs.

"Open them both please Freddie," said Tom. Tom was a great admirer of Freddie's wines especially when he made the more unusual ones. He believed that all mankind lived for sensual pleasure, whether it be drink, food, touch, sex, exercise, smell or taste. He described his life as a series of momentary pleasures. Freddie pulled the cork with a delicious popping noise.

Only Peter remained working. He was bent low over the strawberries picking one and eating one. The juices smearing his lips and turning them from pink to red. He had already filled four punnets and was going to give them to his sister when she picked him up later that evening. He felt his way around each plant until he found a large strawberry and picked it; he left the smaller ones because they were probably green and not yet ready. But the big bulbous fruits were ready and were deliciously sweet. He held each one by its stalk and cap then bit in juicily and then discarded the top over his shoulder. As he edged from plant to plant, he left a train of knee prints in the soil and half eaten strawberries. The birds will have them, he thought.

Tom announced a few minutes later as Billie Holiday sang

> *I see your face in every flower*
> *Your eyes in stars above*
> *It's just the thought of you*
> *The very thought of you, my love*

"I think I am as serious as I have ever been about anything that I have ever done" said Tom, lifting a cup of nettle wine to his lips. "I have had enough of sitting back and watching the country go to hell in a hand cart. I am tired of the little people being trodden down; the government doesn't care about anyone. I look back over my life and the poor are still poor and the rich are still rich and to be honest the poor are getting poorer. The jobs are gone, the miners are on strike to save their livelihoods and their homes and towns. Always believed that things would get better, but really for some they have not. Churchill had an ink stamp you know. It had on it 'Action This Day'. I feel like a bit of action this day. We can do something about all this. We can get the money and distribute it around the area. Make a few lives better. A bit like winning the pools."

"Action this day, maybe after another damson wine," said Hans.

"If we are giving the money away then I will be with you Tom," said Freddie smiling.

"The church needs a new wiring system and new slates on the roof, and that young woman needs a bit of help too" replied Hans.

Only Greggory did not answer. Hans told them the story of the girl and they nodded quietly, smoked cigarettes and pipes. While they were drinking the nettle and damson wine the world seemed slowly to be on its way to becoming a little better place.

At the end of the story Greggory sighed wearily and said: "We are born and then we live and then we die. It's only what we do in the middle bit that really counts." They all nodded towards him sagely, as if this was the purest wisdom ever spoken.

And so, it was, without realising it quite yet, that the Allotment Gang was formed; it had a philosophy and a credo, but as yet no plan. It may, at this point, have been the wine talking at the end of a long day of labour, but in Tom's mind he had validation for his new world view. For the others it was simply the wine talking, though Hans and Freddie liked very much the idea of some new adventure in their lives.

The next morning, Tom walked down to the church. He had a nice bunch of sweet peas in his hands, wrapped in brown paper. At the latch gate, the bell of St Mary the Virgin's rang out, a single solemn tone. The grass was overgrown and the paths needed weeding. Tom made a mental note to come back the next day with an edging fork to sort this out and some weed killer for the pebbled path. He crunched his way up to the main door of the Nave and turned right and walked through into the graveyard, passing the stones of the great and the good and the loved and lost of the parish for more than two hundred years. He passed the stones of those whose names had long been forgotten. Whose stones were so damaged that barely an outline could be made of the memory of who they once were and when they had lived. The first stone that could be deciphered was 'Edward Tully, late of this parish died 1832 Farmer and soldier.' Further down the grass path he arrived at the newer internments. He continued across the lawn until he stopped at a simple black stone, where his wife lay for the past three years.

Loss is a terrible thing. Grief had descended on Tom like a sooty cloud blotting the sunshine out of his life. Grief was a part of his everyday life; it would not go away. It became a constant companion. He could not blot the sadness out of his head. He returned to her in his mind every minute of every hour of every day for a year and then, when he was at his lowest and the world of happiness and pleasure was lost to him, he contemplated joining her. He had bought a double plot in the graveyard so eventually his essence would mix with hers beneath the grass. They too would be too soon forgotten and cast from the memories of the living by death and time itself. He drank heavily and wept in the most inconvenient and embarrassing of places. But James the vicar came to see him. They had been friends for a long time. James did not have to say anything. He was just a companion at first. He did not have to say anything because nothing that could be said would make any sense of the trauma of losing a wife of forty-five years. James had always preached about the importance of silence in everyday life. Being quiet was in the bible. He would say after a period of quiet and reflection we should clothe ourselves each day with our best clothes to make us look ready for the world. Then once we were dressed in our best clothes, we should clothe ourselves in kindness, compassion and humility. Only then would we be ready to go out and deal with the world. So, quietness came easy to James, who always gave off an aura of saintliness, tranquillity and peace. An aura that Tom needed to wrap round him at that time. As the weeks became months, James comforted Tom with both silence and kind words. It helped him compress the pain and the suffering so it became a smaller and smaller part of each day.

Tom placed the flowers on the grave in a little jam jar that was embedded in the earth at the foot of the black polished stone. He sat down and told his wife the story of the girl. He tidied up the edging with a trowel and some garden scissors.

As Tom left the graveside, he spotted Rev James putting up notices on the parish notice board. He was dressed in blue jeans and a pink shirt. Only real men wear pink, Tom thought, remembering the comment his daughter had once made to him.

"Morning vicar," said Tom.

"Oh, good afternoon, Tom, how are you? Have you been visiting?"

"Yes, I will be back tomorrow to put some weed killer on the path here if that is ok with you? I may tidy up the grass borders too."

Reverend James was a fat man. There is no other way of saying it. He had jowls that wobbled when he spoke. His voice was deep and throaty and he was quick to smile. His sizable belly hung over his thin hips and his pink shirt sat out in front of him like a tent. A small child could have sheltered from the rain beneath its shroud. He had a full head of hair which was long on top and swept back like a posh public-school boy. Two strands always hung across his forehead no matter how much it was combed. James had been the vicar for twenty years, having served his time in an inner-city parish helping some of the poorest people with terrible lives and lifestyles. He would tell you it wore him down and when he was offered the opportunity to come out to a rural parish, he had seized the chance and had quickly settled into village life. He liked the bring and buy, the Saturday coffee mornings, visiting the elderly and giving talks to the steam train society of which he was secretary. In fact, railway memorabilia was his passion and when he had first arrived at the church he was delighted to discover the graves of three railway men who had been killed in a boiler explosion 102 years before. The grave stones had pictures of locomotives on them and stood together as a memory of the team the men had once been. James had lovingly restored these and they had become a small feature that brought railway enthusiasts to the church in the same way the grave of a famous writer or musician would. Scattered around the church were old station benches with the GNR or GWR logo on them. The village station name was on the wall in the presbytery a reminder of the line taken by Dr Beacham and now restored as a cycle path. A few items of his railway collection had found their way into the Star Lane allotment toilet block. James was a man of great humour and winning smiles. But today Tom thought he looked a little glum. His shoulders were hunched and he, unusually, had a look of concern on his face.

"Are you ok James?" said Tom.

"Oh, you know a few things on my mind. We are having problems with the electrics and I am afraid we will need to rewire this old place sooner rather than later. I worry about a fire starting. It's an expensive process Tom. I have tried prayer but I think He has more pressing concerns at the moment." James smiled that easy smile that made him so well liked in the village.

"Yes, Hans mentioned it to me last night," said Tom.

"I had a quote from Bill Smith, but it was £3000 which is way out of the reach of the diocese at present. They prefer to spend the money they have on the poor. Far more Christian I believe." James smiled again. He had the uncanny ability to light up a room with his charm, Tom thought.

"I will be starting a fundraiser, but we will need to sell a few cakes and teas to raise that sort of money. However, we have done it before to help this old building." James said with feeling as he slapped the palm of his hand affectionately against the stone wall.

If you are passing the library on your way home Tom, would you mind asking them to put one of these up?" James handed over a "banda" newsletter. It smelled still of alcohol and all the writing was in blue.

"But of course, James. Here give me a few more. I will post them on the wall of the pub and shop too."

Peter's diary

The days drift into one. I don't know what day it is today. I have odd rhythms to my life now that I am forced into a retirement. Yet I do not want to retire from the world or lose sight of what day it is. But retirement is like a permanent holiday. All the free time that I wished for when I was working has been delivered to me now. And yet I still have to work hard not to fall into the trap of ennui and sit silently on the sofa for an unwanted hour. I remember that the 18th of January was always designated as the worst day of the year because it is in January which is always a bad month, it is after the joys of Christmas and it is ahead of the first pay package of the year and it's when the credit card bills arrive. Keeping on top of my own mental wellbeing really comes down to me. Planning and lists. I used to love writing lists. Sometimes I would write something I'd already done onto my list just so I could immediately cross it off. But lists can't be seen any more so I have to store them in my head. I find everything so dull with the exception of the allotment. There all my senses move into overload and I can gain a great sense of happiness in this.

Chapter Three

In the far corner of the field of allotments stood the formidable shape of Rosie Hamilton, now in her late 60s she looked like a woman half her age. Her strong arms were folded across a sizable chest, wrapped in a red polka dot shirt. She wore blue dungarees and lurid pink wellington boots. She had a look of deep concentration on her face. She always had that look on her face and it was often misinterpreted as looking cross by those who did not know or like her. Rosie was not cross about anything. She would tell you that she did not do anger and then with an enormous sonorous laugh, that she only did revenge. She had that rare disposition of a permanently jolly and friendly person. Some would say salt of the earth or a larger-than-life character, but she would never let anyone describe her as bubbly. She despised that description. Her father used to bring home young gentlemen to attempt, as Rosie believed, to get her off his hands. She remembered hearing him describing her to various suitors as bubbly and friendly and once much worse, having good child bearing hips. Rosie would make a great effort to reject every one of her father's choices for marriage. The look on her face this morning was generated by thoughts about current form and future formation. She wanted her vegetables not to be shaded by her runner beans that were currently only just a few inches high, but would grow up the bamboo wigwams and potentially put her tomatoes into shade. Everyone knows that tomatoes need sunshine to ripen, otherwise she would be making green chutneys again this year. Rosie was not one to make the same mistake twice.

As the sun rose, she worked hard on her patch. She wielded a shovel and a hoe with muscular aplomb. She could arm wrestle any of the men on the allotment and in one of the rare moments when she decided to join in the end of day wine drinking, she would often be challenged to an arm wrestle. A challenge that she enjoyed because she liked to put the silly old fools in their place. Rosie was the go-to person to fix things in the village. During the war she had been a Land Girl and had become a vehicle mechanic. She could take an America deuce and a half truck apart and put it back together in a better condition than when she started. Her love of all things mechanical was well known in the village and people would bring her broken toasters, hoovers and washing machines to repair. She had even managed to repair the broken neck on a banjo and reconstruct a working hurdy-gurdy.

It did not matter where Rosie was or what she was doing, whether it was gardening or draining the oil out of an engine or at the vicar's garden party, she always wore thick red lipstick. She told all her friends that when she died she wanted everyone to wear red lippy at her funeral, she would slap her hip and say "especially the fellas."

Rosie had had an interesting and full life. She was the granddaughter of a Marquis; her grandmother had been a house maid in his service. Once the pregnancy had been discovered her grandmother was shipped off to Cornwall with a handsome yearly stipend. Her mother had been born into middle class wealth and had later married a school teacher who had also inherited well. Rosie in her turn had been born a bright and able child who went on to read languages at Manchester University. She was starting her third year when the war started and she volunteered immediately to help on the land. A woman scholar was still a rare sight in Manchester before the war and a rarer sight taking a jeep apart during it. Her unfinished degree was of some use since she was discovered as a Land Girl to have a good knowledge of German and had been sent to work at Bletchley Park. Here she worked on translating German U boat messages after they had been decoded. She had in 1945 joined SOE and while in training the war had ended. After the war she had married and had five children, her husband died in the early 70s and she had returned to work translating novels from German to English for a Birmingham publishing house. She had arrived astride a Triumph Bonneville at the Star Lane allotments five years before, dressed from head to toe in black leathers and a white silk scarf. She had been accepted immediately by the Allotment Allocation Committee. Not many people turned Rosie down. She was often seen on her patch working and she could be heard singing to herself and more often talking to herself. Rosie kept bees and she had four hives at the far end of the site. "They keep everything working in these allotments just like a splash of oil" she would say.

Freddie Lancaster's allotment was full sized and Freddie regarded it as his pride and joy and his full-time job. Freddie is a tall angular man with a ramrod straight back. He had silver grey hair and wore a pince-nez above a large moustache. His face was of near perfect complexion for a man and he was very handsome. He looked like a man who ate sparingly and lived a frugal life, but he was not that man. The edges of his pockets were hanging on his jacket, his elbows had patches and his trousers looked so worn at the knees, that there was barely any cloth between the outside world and his skin. He wore a dapper red cravat at his neck and his shirt was always open due to missing buttons. His wife called this look 'Freddie in his scruff'. After years of working in a suit he delighted in the freedom of the scruff. Freddie's allotment was in no way a reflection of his sartorial standards for Freddie was a show gardener. He grew for competition and aimed always for the largest and heaviest individual plants and crops. His allotment was shaped like a union jack with a central cross walkway and then smaller paths running diagonally across the centre. At the centre grew huge sunflowers, tall and ungainly with moon flowers pointing always towards the sunshine. In each of the triangular beds grew a different crop of show vegetables. There were fewer plants in each section than in the more prosperous parts of the field. But these plants were often of ridiculous and inedible proportions. Super-size marrows, turnips, tomatoes and onions littered the bays.

When Freddie showed he looked like a different man. The flamboyance of the ex-RAF officer came out. Hand stitched tweed suits, dapper shoes, gold pocket watches, a lethal looking knobkerrie walking stick and splendid pork pie straw hats gave him the air of a dandy. The transformation was remarkable and his elegance made him a bit of a star of the horticultural circuit. He had appeared on several occasions on television. He would often arrive at shows on his old Velocette Venom 500cc motorbike with his prize vegetables sat in a sidecar. But this was all an affectation. Freddie was as down to earth as anyone on the scene but he realised that this small eccentricity got him more noticed by the judges. It was all part of the great game he would say. It may even have distracted the judges from the occasional small flaw in his prize-winning vegetables and flowers.

Freddie believed that his greatest ever purchase was a blue and white striped hammock with two slats of wood at either end to keep it from curling around the recumbent. It was attached between an apple and plum tree and on lazy summer days and after working the soil, he thought there was no better place to be on God's earth. The other gardeners watched enviously as Freddie could be seen eyes closed below a cocked fedora or pork pie hat, a pipe in his mouth with smoke emanating wistfully from the bowl and a copy of a novel lazing on his chest. He had placed an old metal garden table within reach of the hammock. On this often sat, a cup of filter coffee or a large Gin and Tonic. Freddie called this spot Tranquillity Base after the moon landing site.

Across his chest lay an open copy of Tom Sawyer and Huckleberry Finn. Freddie preferred the classics and considered, in that old-fashioned way, that being well read was a gentlemanly thing to be. His old house master had told him so in the 1930s, but had also said that it would give him something to talk to girls about when he went up to Oxford. However, in his last term he had joined the RAF after one of those very women, who he enchanted with his ability to recite poetry and extracts from Andrew Marvell and Henry Vaughan, had observed that the RAF uniform made a man stand out from a crowd. Within four months he was in a Hawker Hurricane over the South Downs hunting Heinkel bombers. Shot down twice, he never forgave the woman he met at Oxford, but kept his love for a good book to this day.

In the evening, as the shadows stretched across the allotments and the throbbing summer heat began to leave the soil Freddie liked to meet up under the central pergola, that stretched between the three central sheds. Here there was a time to relax and rub away the aches and strains of the day. There was always a smell of Deep Heat which was never quite smothered by the smell of vines and wisteria, that hung from the trellis. In the winter this was a woody knot of branches and runners. But on a warm sunny

August evening, it felt a little like sitting in Tuscany. Under the pergola, there was a large rectangular table made from railway sleepers and benches running parallel on both sides. Hans had a fridge and from it a bottle of Riesling would often appear or one of Freddie's homemade wines. The men enjoyed the silence of the Worcestershire countryside all day, but in the communal early evening meetings an old record player would play Count Basie, Bird, Cab Calloway, Glen Miller, Dizzy, Sinatra or Bing. Music is most important to people when they are young, it imprints a moment on the memory which travels with them for a lifetime. You can remember a time, a person and a place just with the first few bars of a song or a melody. People rarely move their tastes on from the time of their youth. They returned to the sounds of their teens and twenties and the men sat round the table were no different. There was always a chess board set up at one end of the table and the two tiny clocks which you punch with the palm of your hand to stop matches running into hours and days. At the side of the main table are some work spaces for potting up or for dealing with cuttings. A single factory light in green enamel swings above the table along with two old hurricane oil lamps. Next to the door of the shed was a chalk board with a list of jobs that needed doing. Freddie believed that making lists was the best part of the day. Planning was everything in gardening. Just like Peter, Freddie often said nothing gave him more pleasure than ticking off a job on a list. Chalked up today was:

1. Water beds.
2. Prick out the tomatoes.
3. Hoe beds 1-3.
4. Compost bins!
5. Write a letter to David.

It was number five that Freddie was now engaged in. Slumped over the table with a fountain pen. He, like many of his generation, had wonderful handwriting. Next to him Greggory was painting a flower in water colours. The flower sat in an old milk bottle and Greggory was using a little travel watercolour set to paint. He had a look of intense pleasure on his face. For indeed this was a place of happiness, peace, friendship and tranquillity.

At the other end of the table Tom and Hans were playing their daily chess game. Hans was feeling a little irritated because, after every few moves Hans, made Tom would announce that it was part of some chess masters move.

"Queen to knight 6. Ah! the Kasparov conjecture."

There was no Kasparov conjecture, but Tom liked to wind Hans up when he knew he was going to lose again. In ten years, he had only beaten Hans a handful of times. But this did not deter his endeavours, for he believed that the only way to get better was to play someone better. To date he could not see the improvement.

Without looking up from the chess game Tom announced: "Hans and I have decided we are going to rob the Post office at Chaddesley and then give the money to the vicar so he can fix the church and distribute it to the poor and needy. Who's in?"

"Yeah, right you crazy guys. Have you been on the wine since yesterday?" said Greggory

"Nope, we are absolutely serious." Hans replied not looking up from the chess board.

The painting and letter writing continued and silence descended across these peaceful endeavours. After a while Freddie broke the silence.

"Is this some sort of joke?"

"No, we are quite serious. We just thought you two ex-war heroes, standing all day up to your boot rims in horse manure, would be interested in a little Robin Hood."

"Ok, what's the plan?" said Greggory, not quite believing what he was hearing but happy to listen. He twirled the water colour brush in a jam jar of discoloured water. Freddie wearily put down the newspaper and leaned forward. "Ok what's the plan?"

Tom and Hans laughed and Tom said: "I have no idea."

It took them a couple of days but Hans and Tom came up with a plan. They would raid the Post Office at Chaddesley. Hans and Tom would drive to the Post office in a car that would be borrowed and rested in the lock up at the edge of the allotment until required. They would go into the Post Office just before closing time and would be in disguise in blue boiler suits and balaclavas. A lot of factory workers dressed like this so they would not seem out of the ordinary, just two blokes walking home from work. A stocking pulled over their faces would add to the disguise. One would carry an old rusty shotgun found in one of the sheds years before which would be cleaned up to look serviceable. The other would carry an old service pistol, unloaded. The pistol had been smuggled through Liverpool docks when Tom had returned home and was demobbed from the war in 1945. It had been a risk to conceal back then and it would be a 25-year prison risk to carry it now. Greggory had been in the Post Office and had drawn a plan of where everything was and noted the CCTV camera above the man who worked each day behind the glass screen. To ensure there would be no police nearby Greggory would follow the local policeman during the raid and Freddie would be by the phone box round the corner should Greggory call, and then use his motorbike to get a warning to them with three blasts on the horn. They doubted the rural beat officer would turn up during the raid. There would not be another policeman within ten miles. They set about earnestly to prepare.

*

Three weeks later, they were ready. The night before the raid Tom and Hans sat in Tom's car in a suburb of Birmingham at 2am in the morning drinking strong black sugary coffee from a thermos flask to keep them alert. The tree lined street was silent but for the hoot of an owl and a distant bark of a city fox. It was an affluent middle-class area so everyone was asleep ahead of work in the morning. They had driven past a cul de sac and had seen a blue and white Mini parked up on the pathway against a tall hedge. The owner would regret blocking the pathway, forcing people with prams onto the road. This little piece of selfishness did not go unmissed in selecting a car for the raid. There were so many Minis in the area it made the perfect inconspicuous vehicle for a robbery. Tom and Hans were ready. Hans stepped out of the car and Tom drove off. Hans waited for a few moments to see if any lights went on or curtains twitched and then walked back down the road and turned right into the small cul de sac. Edging himself along the wet hedge he arrived at the door of the car. From out of his pocket, he produced a long 12-inch piece of metal with a hooked end and forced it down through the window and into the interior of the door. A short tug upwards and the lock was lifted and the door opened. The principles of hot wiring a car is fairly straight forward and once learned are not forgotten. Hans had the wires off and touched them together in seconds and the car came to life with the sound of the 1000cc engine.

A quick look around and he drove the car out of the cul de sac putting the lights on once around the corner. The whole enterprise from leaving Tom's car to driving away had taken less than four minutes. The car was in the old lock up garage next to the disused Star Inn inside of three quarters of an hour. Tom was waiting with a new set of license plates and the car was almost ready for use.

The next morning, a small allotment fire was prepared. Two old boiler suits were found, the Mini received a loving service and a change of oil. Rosie had been brought in to help service the car, though she was told that Greggory was just doing a favour for a friend. She was not to be involved in the robbery but her expertise enabled the mini to be reliable and quick. For her part Rosie liked working with cars and she liked working with Greggory more. A fake Tax disc was drawn and placed in the window. The old Velocette and sidecar was similarly looked over with care. Freddie was to follow the car on his bike. Tom found a pair of old stockings in his wife's closet. They decided who was to talk and who was to stay watch at the door.

The day passed quietly. The jobs of the allotment proceeded as normal. Crops were watered. The bees were smoked from one of their hives and a quantity of honey comb was recovered. Weeding and hoeing proceeded at a back breaking pace for no one liked weeding; the job is tedious and needs to be completed as quickly as possible. Tomato plants were sprayed for aphids and the bird feeders were filled once again with seeds and nuts. At lunch the gang sat with cheese rolls and mugs of tea and contemplated life and the rich beauty of Peter's gardening.

By the morning of the raid all was ready. They sat and waited.

"Do we need the guns, Hans?"

"Yes, we need them to show that we are proper gangsters, not amateurs."

"You know that means 25 years if we get caught." said Tom. "I've not got 25 left in me."

"Better not get caught then," said Hans.

"We lived through the greatest historical calamity of the century, played our parts albeit on different sides of the tragedy and do you know there is no record of our role in the history books. It is a common lament from ordinary people like ourselves. So, if we get caught, we will make it into the newspapers at least, if not the history books."

"The adventure will be enough for me." said Hans.

Peter's diary

I can't read these pages back to myself. Not sure at all why I bother to write these diaries. Loneliness, boredom? There is nothing so challenging to life than the tyranny of the empty page. Even if I cannot actually see it. The white paper still shouts out what have you done? Fill the page to make my life in some way important, to give it value. Maybe someone else will read these and will find solace. Or maybe these ramblings will end up in a skip and then landfill.

There seems to be some sort of commotion today. There was a lot of coming and going and I was working during the day which is unusual for me. From the sound of their working, I could hear that the men were anxious. There were lots of rapid strokes of the hoe. Lots of sighing and vigorous cutting and paring back of plants and bushes. Their rhythms of work were all not quite right. My friends on the allotment are feeling distressed. Maybe the time of harvest is stressful. Getting it just right not damaging or ruining all the work that has already been put in over the years. I listen in to conversations and do so because my blindness has made me invisible to all. People don't see me in the same way as I don't see them. They don't know that I was a teacher once. I taught philosophy and so when I heard them discussing what it is to be a good man or to lead a good life I am always drawn to these questions.

Chapter Four

The plan was simple and worked on the principle that they knew the only policeman within ten miles was a rural officer who finished work at 2pm on a Friday and was well known to tour the local pubs checking on licencing issues but really having a pint in the back room with each landlord. He'd then leave the Mini Countryman patrol car in the Queens Head pub car park where his wife would meet him and drive him home. As long as someone followed Sergeant Brian Redcarr from 12 -2pm they would be free of any response from the police. So, at 1.30pm Greggory sat in the Boars Head, one eye on the police car through the public bar window while nursing a "Banks's" bitter shandy, his third of the morning so far. Sergeant Brian was already garrulous and filled with unusual bonhomie for a man who was normally taciturn. He had done his 39 years and had been farmed out to the rural beat and he was happy with that. He had one more year and he did not want to spend it booking in foul mouthed yobs in the big stations in Birmingham. He had been there and done that as he would tell you, if you were prepared to listen. Now he wanted an easy life. Gregory shifted on his seat so he could see into the back of the bar where Sergeant Brian was standing next to the dishwasher boy drinking a pint and chatting to the publican. Gregory was to ring Freddie at the phone box if the sergeant deviated from his routine. If he could not get through to the phone box, he would invent some sort of incident or feign a heart attack and so keep the officer busy. The sergeant was not the best of detectives and had failed to notice the same small West Indian man dressed in a pin striped suit and a Wailers t-shirt in the previous two pubs had been drinking in. Maybe that's why he was never promoted from being on the beat.

Chaddesley post office sat on the corner of Station Road and opposite the Vernon pub which served hand pulled beers in a time when fizzy keg beer was popular. Mrs Simpson was just about to finish work and could not wait to turn the sign on the door over to 'closed' and get home to watch her favourite soaps. Her son had bought her a VHS recorder and she had a nice bit of chicken left from last night's meal and was going to have that reheated with roast potatoes.

Friday was not her normal day of work. She usually helped out on the busy Saturday mornings but Fred Jones had called in sick that morning and so she had been drafted in to do a full day by herself. It was not a convenient arrangement because she had planned to sort through all the offerings for the church bring and buy sale which was running on Saturday afternoon. Reverend James was always sympathetic to his volunteers not turning up. Mary Simpson was a portly good-natured widower who had a desire to dye her hair all sorts of lurid colours. She said she was 'growing old disgracefully', to anyone who asked why she had such elaborate colouring. She had just finished counting up the cash in her tray and made a note on the pad next to the telephone. She thought she would get ahead of herself and make the totting up quicker at the end of the day. She had £2392.63 in the roll out cash box in front of her. Quite a few people had been paying for car tax and buying premium bonds so she had an unusually large float. An hour before she had considered putting most of it in the large green wall safe behind her and closing the steel door but that sat open with a further £1500 in foreign currency mostly US dollars ordered in for Mr and Mrs Smith's once in a lifetime trip to Florida in a weeks' time. She envied the Smiths. Still married and happy with each other in retirement. She had hoped that her Sam would have had the same life experiences but he had died several years before, swept away by a simple winter flu that had become pneumonia and taken him from her at 64. A year before he was to retire from the great steel presses at the big Garringtons drop-forge factory complex. The ones that boomed through the night stopping small children from getting to sleep in the light nights of summer.

The post office door creaked open, the bell chimed a welcoming tinkle and in stepped Hans and Tom, dressed in identical blue boiler suits, heavy workmen's boots, leather gloves with stockings and a balaclava over their heads. Mrs Simpson seemed thrilled to see them. She was about to have the most exciting thing happen to her since she had snorkelled on a reef in Australia and a large turtle had passed her close enough to her so she could reach out and touch its slime covered shell. Her heart pounded a little as the adrenalin in her body increased with the thrill of a real-life robbery. She was not a woman normally fazed by much and her first reaction was to think about what the ladies at the WI would think when she told them and would she get on the local news that night. She was anything but quick moving and while the second thought to pass through her head was to kick the safe door closed, she was not as quick as Hans, who had crossed through the shop past rows of stationery and birthday cards and had arrived at the plate window. He was carrying an old service revolver which had no bullets in it. The plan was to allow Tom to arrive at the same time and simply ask to hand over the money calmy. But the excitement had got the better of him and so had a realisation that the lady before him attended the same church.

He called out: "Hand over zer money in der till!" his Austrian accent provocatively on full display.

A hush descended as all three people in the conversation realised who each other was.

"Hand over the cash from the till please love," said Tom.

Mrs Simpson harrumphed her disapproval that the man she had stared at across the church for the past five years and had been her sole desire since she had seen him for the first time ten years before was now wearing a stocking on his head and was robbing the post office.

"Some men go to extraordinary lengths to impress," She exclaimed while stuffing the sack with cash, her face a mixture of contempt and desire. The notes were pushed deeply into the sack until they spilled out of the top. It was a lot of money and a small sack.

By now Tom was at the door lifting the blinds to stare outside and check the street which was empty.

"Don't say anything" Hans pleaded under his breath

"Well, it depends, doesn't it," Mrs Simpson purred.

"What does it depend on?"

"Well, I expect you at my house on Saturday night preferably with flowers, chocolate and wine." She said with a coyness belying her years and life experiences. "That's the price of silence, Herr Doktor Schmitt." She rolled the words playfully.

"It's a deal I can explain everything," said Hans, snatching the bag of money and running to the door.

Mrs Simpson fell back into her chair and sighed. When the police looked at the CCTV much later it looked like she had swooned. She certainly had, but not with the shock of the robbery but with the thrill of it all and the prospect of an evening with a German paratrooper, doctor of medicine and bank robber. Nothing as good as this had happened in Chaddesley Corbett for a long time. Nothing as good as this had happened to Mrs Simpson for years either. Now she was a bank robber's Moll, or at least intended to be.

They exited the Post Office running down the cobbled alley next to the main street. They arrived at the car while stripping the stockings off their heads. The car started with the first twist of the loose wires. They drove off elated.

"Will she tell?" shouted Tom.

"No, I've done a deal."

"A deal?"

"Yes, don't worry the police will not be coming for us both just yet." Hans sounded reassuring.

"I bloody hope so. You and your Kraut accent. I said I'd do all the talking."

"Less of the Kraut!"

"I've not felt that scared since crossing the Chindwin river in 1944," Tom roared, over compensating for the noise of the newly turbo charged engine.

Within ten minutes they were driving the car into the allotment garage where it had sat for years. Then they burned all the clothes on the already stoked fire that Greggory had made when he returned from observing the police and his afternoon drinking. A fire of old timber and brambles was burning and the boiler suits, balaclavas, stockings and gloves were thrown on to make the first smoke before the pieces burned to cinders.

That night the Mini was returned to the same street with the original number plates, except it was parked on the road and not the pavement and was in far better condition than it had been when it was borrowed. The sound of the Velocette and sidecar did wake one of the neighbours as it drove away, but the neighbour thought nothing of it and went downstairs to make a glass of warm milk and to pet the purring cat. Once home, Tom put £500 in an old Co-op plastic bag and wrapped it round the door handle of the young woman's bungalow opposite. He pushed a note through the door saying that Jenny should look in the bag and look after her baby. At the same time, Hans posted the rest of the money inside a thick brown envelope, through the door of the rectory. He turned and walked back down the path as silent as a cat with a smile etched across his face. His only thought now was an evening with Mrs Simpson.

Peter's diary

I was waiting to be picked up and had been forgotten again this evening. I am guessing completely forgotten and that a car would screech to a halt in the next hour or I would sleep on this bench. It will not be the first time I have slept here, woken twice by foxes snuffling by and once by the sound of a badger gorging themselves on fallen apples. I have learned to leave a bucket of bruised apples out but I have to do this secretly because the others don't like the badger in the allotments. So, I place the bucket on the other side of the wire near the chickens. There was a little nonsense going on earlier as Tom and Hans arrived on the motorbike. They had left separately. I am not sure what was going on but they sounded very pleased with themselves and were giggling like two young boys. "The age of miracles has not passed", said Tom mysteriously and then they both fell about and went off to their homes. When I tell people that I keep a diary their first reaction is to ask if it is in Braille. The second is what do I find to write about. Today in a moment of gloominess in the library, Marianne said that I should write something good that happened to me each day.

Finding happiness in the ordinary is a regular theme in philosophy. So today I managed to lie down between the lettuce and the beans and without someone coming up and kicking the soles of my feet to see if I was still alive. This allowed me to just listen. They have all now got used to me listening to the world- it disconcerted them for a while mainly because they thought I'd collapsed or had a stroke. But being on my back with my face to the sky is one of the great joys in life. Simply concentrating on listening is not what most people have time to do. They are always too busy or there are too many distractions in life. But to lie on the soil and listen to the world around you is very pleasing. The bird song alone is worth the effort of stillness. The starlings in particular make an awful bubbling racket when they are socialising. A conversation of bubbles and squeaks that is strangely reassuring to both me and the birds. Then there is the peep of the house martins as they flash overhead. There are several very fat pigeons that coo noisily away. Monty the cat has his eye on them and I can hear him rustling through the allotment. He will get one soon. When the fly they make a whumping sound like helicopter blades. Today the slight breeze from the west brought me the sound of Eleanor playing her cello. Eleanor's parents are the nearest neighbours to the allotments and I could hear the Bach cello piece that I've always liked. She is quite a talent for a sixteen-year-old girl. She seems to have mastered the rhythms and nuances of the music. Further off a tractor interrupted the melody and a light airplane flew down the valley some way off. Freddie told me it was a Cessna and asked me later if I would clean up and oil the old shotgun that he'd found in his shed a few years ago. He managed to get the rust off it and needed it to be oiled and polished. I said I'd help him but was unsure it would work again. My father had guns so I know how to handle and clean them. Freddie said if we could get it working it would sort out the rat and rabbit problems, we had all been having. So, I spent a couple of hours cleaning it up for him. Later I could hear the sawing of metal from his shed.

Chapter Five

Tom woke to the news that there was no news. He had often thought that his life would be so much better if he never heard the news. What you don't hear you can't worry about and so little of the real world of politics and international affairs ever reached this small sleepy village. His friend from church, Marianne, had said she refused to watch the news or read a newspaper and that she had stopped during the Falklands War. Her life was richer for it and her mental health was better for it too. Almost all her knowledge of worldly events came from an amusing Disc Jockey of Radio 2. His endless cheerfulness was a boon to her life and kept her on a steady keel. As for newspapers, she believed they will be gone in twenty years. Feeding the people sensationalism, fear, prejudice and pointless celebrity gossip was not a good or sustainable economic model. Marianne was a woman of privilege and lived as a wealthy widow in the big house on the corner opposite the village library and café. She volunteered in the library five days a week and knew everyone who came in by name and quite extraordinarily she could remember which books many of the elderly people had read before and could advise them not to take out stories they had already read. For some she was the only person they would speak to over several days and she relished in keeping her elderly and often lonely clientele in over long conversations about their lives and the things they had been doing. The library was being threatened with closure as a cost cutting exercise by the council. Tom liked books but he liked Marianne even more and knew how much the library meant to her and the community. Himself included.

The radio did not report the robbery, and for a few days there seemed to be no activity and it was quickly a non-story. But actually, there was activity going on behind a media fog. Two detectives called Hunter and Savage had been on the scene the very next morning. Sent in from the city because the Superintendent had little faith that a village bobby would be able to deal with such matters. It was after all an armed robbery and CID should be involved. Detective constable Mike Savage was a graduate of Birmingham University with a degree in History and Art History. He was seen as competent and astute by senior staff who marked him out for quick promotion. After his two years on the beat, he had been moved to the CID to help progress a fledgling career. He was short with scraggy long hair and a little overweight from fast food meals sat in cars on endless surveillance of gangland Birmingham. At just 24 years old he believed himself to be a superhero in the same way that the red-braced shouting traders that he watched on the news, and who seemed to be hoovering up money, believed themselves to be indestructible. Mike Savage was affable and cynical beyond his years. He had a good mind but he was lazy. He liked sitting in cars and not wearing fussy uniforms. He had grown his hair long just as the fashions of the 1980s had moved to short haircuts. He listened to Led Zeppelin and Pink Floyd when the rest of his generation were listening to Wham, Duran Duran and Spandau Ballet. He had grandpa collared shirts and corduroy jeans and cowboy boots. He would look out of place anywhere, in any time and in any company. But what Mike Savage had that few policemen had at that time was a university degree and it also helped that his father was the Chief constable of Merseyside. In contrast Detective sergeant Derek Hunter was a police lifer and had worked his way up the greasy pole of success and status through hard work and determination. A real accomplishment since he lacked intelligence and judgement in equal proportions. What he did have was a predisposition to violence and an extraordinary ability to cover up his errors and place blame on someone else's doorstep. As a result, he was unpopular among his colleagues who regarded him as someone promoted out of the range of his abilities. As a part of the unit that investigated Birmingham gangsters, he had used his limited skills, liberal use of violence, and an ability to deposit evidence on suspects to secure a conviction. The gangsters themselves hated him because he always got one of them, though not necessarily the right one of them, for that particular crime. That morning the superintendent had asked him to look at a minor robbery in Worcestershire on the grounds that it was close to their force area and was probably one of the local mobsters. Almost immediately he had driven from the meeting to Jack Large's house in Aston. Jack was a local small-time villain who was known to have recently purchased a sawn-off shotgun. Hunter knew Large from old and had jailed him more than once. He saw an immediate visit to this suspect's home as a quick win on the case. Jack Large was a suspect because a sawn-off had been used. Large had just got one. Large was a villain. Case closed. It was policing at its very finest or so Hunter thought.

Arriving at the house Hunter had put on thick black gloves and told Savage to wait by the car. Savage watched him walk up the garden path of a non-descript council-owned semi-detached house. The house next door was boarded up and covered in graffiti. The word 'Nonce' was written in red letters across the door. It was ten o'clock in the morning and no one was around when he pushed the doorbell. Jack Large in boxer shorts and a Motorhead t-shirt stretched across a fulsome beer belly opened the door to be greeted by a sharp punch in the face. He fell backward into the small hallway. Hunter worked on the principle that no one would believe anything Large would say, plus Large was a proper criminal and knew how proper policing worked.

"Where were you yesterday?" Hunter shouted into the face of Large.

"I was here Sergeant Hunter!" said Large, gripping his already bleeding nose. "I was here all day. Sat in the back garden on a bender with the missus. We had some friend's round. Whatever happened yesterday I was not involved." Large's alibi came out like a stream of consciousness mixed with speckles of blood.

"How do you know we are investigating something that happened yesterday?" Hunter slapped him before he realised it was a stupid question.

"You have no right to punch me. I will get you sacked. Nothing worse than a bent copper." sobbed Large.

"You were identified, Mr Large" lied Hunter "plus we know you have a new shooter. The very shooter used in the job."

"What job? I was here all day. The Mrs will tell you. Doreen, Doreen," yelled Large. Doreen Large appeared out of the kitchen at the end of the hall. Just as Hunter had put Large up against the wall with his hand on his throat.

'Alright Doreen?" 'said Hunter.

"What have you done to him? What's this all about? Let him go." Hunter let Large go and he slumped forward coughing exaggeratedly and holding his own neck. The blood dripped from his nose.

"He is trying to fit me up. Doreen, tell him I was here all day with you."

"That's right he hasn't been out of the house for three days except to go and get some fags." Doreen barked.

"When was that?"

"This morning. We have been sat in the garden with all this sunshine. Ask the nonce next door. He's been out in his garden too."

Hunter nodded in the direction of the house to Savage, who was leaning against the car smoking and watching his boss assault the suspect again with a slap. Savage went next door and knocked. There was a pause while everyone looked on nervously. The door opened and out stepped a small man in blue denim shorts and the sort of shirt that would be seen on Shakespearean stage actors. The outfit was made more elaborate and confusing by long white socks and a pair of wooden clogs. The man quickly and anxiously confirmed that Large had indeed been sunbathing with his wife all the previous afternoon. The two neighbours nodded at each other across a privet hedge before going back inside and closing the door on Savage.

Savage returned to the house next door "In the garden all day yesterday Boss" he said to Hunter. Hunter on hearing the news turned on his heels and stormed from the house walking down the weed riddled garden path and got in the car silently and sullenly. Doreen Large followed him shouting until she stopped at the green gate wedged open by a brick. She thought for a moment about throwing the brick at the police car but thought better of it.

"Filthy pig, filthy bent copper pig."

Savage got into the driver's seat of the little blue and white Austin 1100. He turned the ignition key and drove off with the shouts and screams ringing in his ears.

"Well, that is disappointing," mused Hunter.

"No fingerprints, an unreliable elderly witness, good disguises, no trace on the vehicles used, in and out in less than three minutes. No one on the street. No link to recognised gangs. The amounts taken are too small for them to be a serious gang from round here," said Savage. "What next Boss?"

"Quiet, I'm thinking," replied Hunter.

Peter's diary

A really flat day-hungover and feeling depressed. The morning was spent shifting a ton of top soil into one of the new raised beds I had made. This required me to dig out the soil and put it into a wheel barrow and then take it across the allotment paths to my new bed. I managed to do this with only once clipping the edge of one of Tom's raised beds. I am pretty good at navigating myself around. I have a map in my head and this is complimented by my smell and sound map. I can hear the change in the sound of the tyre on the brick paths and onto the grass paths. I can smell the compost bins and then the rose both turning points. Rosie said it was an amazing thing to watch me doing. Though she cheekily cheered when I hit the edge of Tom's raised bed. I miss running. I had always been a runner from being a school boy. I think I was the only one who liked cross country in PE lessons. After leaving school I ran at college and it helped me think through the philosophy I was learning there. Many philosophers are walkers, Kierkegaard walked miles every day. Then when I began to teach, I would run at lunchtime. The running exercise kept the weight off me but mostly helped to think life through and kept me from over worrying about stuff. But when my sight was gone, I could not run and I miss it badly. The only exercise I get now is here at the allotments. Shovelling and barrowing a ton of soil helped lift my spirits a little.

Chapter Six

Tom walked into the small village library to see Marianne, the librarian. She had clearly been weeping and her eyeliner was creating a line down one cheek. At first, he was embarrassed to walk in on perhaps some intimate moment of private grief so he walked straight up to one of the bookcases and over his shoulder he said 'Morning Marianne'. The library had three rooms, one filled with books and book cases, a small kitchenette and a toilet. There were two reading desks with four chairs round each. The library building was an old Toll House and was almost a pentagon in shape. Marianne sat at a desk to the right of the door and to the left was a small seating area for children. The main library room has shelves on all the walls and there were two free standing shelves between the two reading desks. Only one other person was there and that was Pete from the Allotments. He was listening to an audio book through big headphones attached to the tape machine.

Marianne was an elegant woman. She was about five foot eight and had auburn hair styled to her shoulders. She had avoided having her hair cut short which was the fashion for older women and she had decided that she would never allow herself to go grey. Not in colouring or in personality. Marianne would dress for any occasion, however small. She would dress to go food shopping. She believed that making an effort maintained her dignity in age and made her noticed still. She was not going to allow herself to disappear as some women preferred. Her Wardrobe was vast and some of her closest friends said that they had never seen her in the same outfit twice. She would spend an hour each morning preparing herself for the day, even if the day was filled with chores, housework or gardening. Marianne always looked good; some would say glamorous. She had a narrow face with big eyes, a clear complexion and full lips. But Marianne's great gift was not her looks but her ability to make everyone she spoke to feel important. She never talked about herself, but would ask lots of questions to the person she was with. There was never any looking over the shoulder or around the room for someone more interesting to talk to. She was focused on the person in front of her and she made that person feel interesting even if they were a monumental bore.

Marianne composed herself and welcomed him: "We have the new Frederick Forsyth in Tom," she said while wiping the smear from her cheek. "I have kept it for you here under the desk. I know how much you like them."

"Thank you, Marianne," said Tom, turning to see that she was wearing the little Dior jacket and black skirt that he liked so much.

"Looking radiant today, Marianne." Tom liked to flirt sometimes outrageously. It was a guilty pleasure but it brought him a little happiness in his lonely days.

"We have had some bad news Tom," she said. "The council is closing us down. I spent the day on the phone to the head librarian who said that this was a done deal. It's the endless cuts, you know. Britain is not doing as well as some people think, and the council budget called for savings and tightening of belts, and it seems we are to be the victim of that."

"That is terrible news Marianne. We are indeed living in difficult times."

"The country has gone to the dogs, pointless wars and now another miners strike," said Marianne.

"You know who I blame?" said Tom.

"Oh, don't get political Tom."

"Why is it that whenever I complain about a Conservative, I am accused of getting political? I *am* political Marianne. There's nothing wrong with that."

"She is doing the best she can do for this country, standing up to the unions and petty South American dictators. The country voted her in because she is strong. The British like strong leaders."

"So did the Germans."

"Let's not squabble Tom, I have to sort out this whole library thing. There is a solution I have been looking at and perhaps you could take off your raging Trot cap and put on your sensible parish councillor hat on." She smiled, and Tom accepted the little dig at his politics with grace.

"What do you suggest?"

"I have done some research. We could set the library up as a private concern. Run it as a community library with volunteer librarians. It would not take much to train up a few volunteers. The running costs are mostly the heating in the winter."

"The building is expensive though. The council could easily sell this as a little shop." Said Tom

"Yes, they could but when I did dome rooting around there are a number of councils who have given these small libraries away to established trusts. If we could persuade our council to do the same, we would create a trust and run the library ourselves."

"What is in it for the council?" Enquired Tom.

"The council maintains what looks like a council service, they cannot be accused of culling libraries and being philistines in the process. It is a win-win political option for them. They don't have to pay for running costs or the librarian's wages. I suppose that's me.' Marianne smiled and shifted on her seat.

"I think it is in the best interests of the village. We could do things other libraries can't do like sell drinks and art work and other stuff like that. If we could get Parish support, we could be away. Tom could you use your influence?"

"Have you calculated the cost?"

Marianne produced a small black writing book and flipped the pages until she found a page filled with numbers.

"No wages, the heating, the telephone, council tax. We would need two thousand pounds a year. I could apply for grants and hope that we could sustain ourselves. Six thousand would see us through the first three years."

"Grants are not that easy to come by and that's a big one."

"I will ask the village clerk to put it on the agenda for the next meeting. I cannot promise you anything but we can try." Tom knew that the parish did not have that sort of money to hand out. He felt the project would be doomed from the start.

"Shall we meet in a few weeks?" Marianne asked.

"How about over breakfast? Marco does great breakfasts," said Tom.

"How lovely, my guilty pleasure is Marco's breakfasts."

"Is it a date?"

"It's not a date Tom. It's a business meeting, but yes of course."

Tom stepped out of the library and looked down the village street. It was a view that had hardly changed over many years. The main road was partially cobbled and the few shops mixed in with large fronted town houses, where once a merchant class would have lived. Several of the houses were still thatched and like most times of the day Tom found he was the only person standing on the street. There were few shops but those that were still in business were themselves remnants of an era before supermarkets. There was a butcher and a grocery. The bakers were run by an all women cooperative and people drove there to buy the many variations on the modern loaf. The last shop was the newsagents which was next door to the small police station. All felt doomed and there was already a for sale sign on the grocers. Tom wondered how long the village would last.

Peter's diary

I had been listening today to a Radio 4 discussion between several worthies about what constitutes a well lived life. It made me think about the effect that fate has on us all. I had spoken to Rosie about Pascal's Wager only the other day. It reminded me of my friend from school Andy. More than twenty years ago now he had been walking home from work, it was a windy day. He was probably thinking about the youth football team he managed or what he was having for his tea. Just the ordinariness of life and living life. In the same way perhaps as I am recounting this story now in my diary. Here sat at the desk. Making sure that I move a sufficient distance down the page so that I am not writing over what I have already written. Never to see the words anyway. Andrew was walking home and a slate fell off a nearby roof, it spun through the air as it fell and hit him heavily on the head causing an internal bleed that killed him several days later in the Cottage Hospital. One day alive and well and living a full life of work, family and friends and then suddenly dead. I have had twenty more years of life than he had already and if I am lucky, I will have many more. I think the point that I am clumsily making is that fate or serendipity or even karma, call it what you like, determines whether you can live a fruitful life. Simply having more time brings with it more experiences and opportunities. I look at my friends on the allotment and they have all seemingly had extraordinary lives. Who would have thought that Greggory born in Trenchtown would end up here in rural Worcestershire? Arriving on the Windrush, a skilled man and walking down that gangway off the ship to a job with the GPO. He said to me once the hardest part was the contrast between what was promised and the reality of British life. All those vile signs saying 'No coloureds, No Irish and No dogs.' He had thought of going back as soon as he saw the first one. But at work his colleagues had taken to him straight away and he had a war record that protected him from the worst of the racism and abuse. He was soon married and then his son Bernie was born and he probably felt the pressure more. The midwife who had helped deliver Bernie was also a Windrush immigrant and had said that sometimes the white women would refuse to be touched by her because she was black. That midwife went on to become the mayor of the town that adopted her. When Andrew and I were at school our headteacher, a rotund Welshman called Williams would end assemblies with a prayer that always finished the same way "Please don't let me grow up to be worthless." He had been one of the rescuers at Aberfan. It had a profound effect on him and his teaching. All those children lost. Please don't let me grow up to be worthless was a sort of philosophy about living life well. I sort of think that was what the programme was all about today.

Chapter Seven

At the far corner of the field was the only allotment that was surrounded by a low picket fence. It was an unnatural enclosure in an open field of cooperation and friendship. Behind the fence was an immaculate set of raised beds, cloches and bamboo stakes supporting a wide variety of beans and sweet peas. It had the look of a country squires garden. It was the only space with an expensive shed that had hot and cold running water and electric lighting. Inside it had a kitchenette and a large double bed. It was owned by a local retired commodities trader called Oswald Griffin, who had moved up from London a couple of years before and lived in the large thatched house near the end of the village with equally imposing hedges some 10ft high, electronic gates and two large Doberman dogs that wandered the gardens and barked at passers-by. Like the house, this allotment said keep out, it even had a beware of the dog sign even though there were no dogs and the only dog on the allotments was the very well-behaved Monty. Mr Griffin, as he preferred to be called, was a deeply private man and employed a gardener to come and dig and grow on his allotment. He did attend and work the soil too, but the majority of the hard work was achieved through cash in hand payment to an equally reclusive and private worker called Sam. Griffin could be seen several evenings a week, sitting on a wicker chair, smoking a cigar, dressed in tweed and wearing Hunter wellington boots. Griffin often wore a flat cap and occasionally a deerstalker, for he did like to shoot and fish and believed that his clothing and kit should always be of the best quality and reflect his status. Griffin had another habit and this was to spend the odd evening in the company of a woman.

His Rolls Royce would purr up to the carpark and he would emerge with two bottles of Moet and a woman half his age or more, who would carry a large Fortrum and Masons picnic basket as she waddled on high heels up the brick paths to the far allotment. They would disappear until the early morning when he was observed dropping the lady in question off at the railway station for the London train. He did not speak to anyone else on the allotment even when he was given a hearty and welcoming good morning. After several months of being blanked the people on the other allotments gave up speaking to him. They observed his comings and goings and also his evening activities with some amusement, but that was as far as it went.

Griffin had gained his allotment by using an old part of his lease agreement on the big house he had bought in the village. One of the parts of the sale was that the house came with an allotment plot. The plot in question had never been used by the previous owner and the owner before had given the allotment land at the Star Inn to the Allotment Committee as a gift in his will as long as one of the gardens remained in the control of the owner of the property. When Griffin's lawyer had informed him of this, he demanded his right to his allotment as the owner of the newly acquired house. This meant that George Keller, who worked the particular plot, was taken off the land much to his and all the other allotment owners' disgust. To add insult to injury George was not taken on as Griffin's proxy gardener. The Allotment Committee had decided when he moved in to be civil to him, but to work to get him off the land and reinstate George. This seemed the only just conclusion to the situation. But money and the law have little connection to justice and George had to put himself on the waiting list for the council owned allotments a mile and a half away.

"Did you see the car, Tom?" Hans asked, looking over towards the little car park.

"The Roller?" Replied Tom looking up from his newspaper and over his half-moon spectacles.

"Yeah, the Roller, and it's got one of those number plates that spells out the person's name. You know OM 1. They cost a fortune to buy, especially with the number 1 in it."

"The world has gone mad." sniffed Tom. "Anyone who spends money on a personalised number, well it shows bad judgement in life. Should be BE11 END."

Hans grinned and Tom who in philosophical mode, continued after casting a wary eye in the direction of the sunbathing business colossus.

"You know I only ever wanted to be a good man, lead a good life, have adventures and fill my time with books, art and the soil. Maybe a little sport and fishing too. Then the war came and although I tried to avoid doing terrible things, those things became too common for my liking and for my soul. And when it was all over my soul felt ruined, that is if, and only if, I gave it a thought. So, I tried to not think about it, cast the memories into a place at the back of my mind. Put them in a box and sit on the lid so that they could not escape. But, like a scab that you feel you need to pick, I would open the box and look at my damaged soul. So, to escape thinking I kept busy and filled my life with work. Keeping busy is very good for the soul. I wonder if that is what Griffin does here."

"I don't know why he winds you up so much," said Hans. "You are lucky you only have to see him a few times a week. He has to be Oswald Griffin for all his life. Imagine that?"

The sound of Ska music heaved its way into the allotment landscape. Prince Buster had started the elderly group of men to break into song and some rather undignified dancing. The six men each with a Rum and Ting in their hands chortled with laughter as they re-lived their success that day. The music was loud and the beat and the snap of the rhythm guitar sent another wave of smiles and laughter from the group. Only Tom sat on the bench nursing a drink. He had a ladybird on the end of his finger and he was looking at it intensely as it moved down into his palm. 'My little beauty' he whispered. Tom heard a faint voice which made him lean outwards from under the pergola and look down the fields in the direction of Mr Griffin's allotment. He could see Griffin with his shirt off, in shorts sat in the wicker chair that was so large it looked like a throne. Griffin's expansive belly hung heavily over the belt of his designer labelled shorts. A cigar rested in the side of his fulsome lips and sunglasses perched on his red sunburned nose. He was the very model of financial and material success. Rumour had it that he would soon get a gong in the honours list. A true captain of industry.

Griffin shouted again. "Turn off that bloody darkie music."

Tom rose from his chair and placed his Rum on the table. He looked calm as he walked towards the end of the allotment. He returned four minutes later pretending to wring his right hand. He turned the sound up on the music player and sat down next to Hans as if nothing had happened. The rest of the men laughed as they swayed to the rhythms as if they too had not a care in the world.

"Hans. Do you know what the difference is between a hedgehog and a Rolls Royce? Tom shouted over the music."

"What?"

"Do you know what the difference is between a hedgehog and a Rolls Royce?"

Hans shrugged.

"The pricks are on the outside of a hedgehog," roared Tom.

At the far end of the garden Mr Griffin lay on his back over his upturned wicker throne with bubbles of blood coming out of his mouth and wondering to himself what had just happened. What had happened was that Tom had gone to have words with Griffin but had been beaten to it. He found Rosie walking away from Griffin's allotment rubbing her hands having just punched Griffin with such force that it had knocked him clear off his chair and backwards into the dirt. She had objected to the racist comment with the same righteousness as she had objected to being greeted by "Hello sweetheart, what can I do for you?"

Rosie had made straight to Greggory and was now dancing with him with a broad smile on her face. Rosie was a good-looking woman and Greggory knew she was one of the few women he would ever know in his life, that he could just be a friend with. Not because Rosie was unattractive, far from it. It was because Rosie was the most extraordinary person he had ever met. Anything other than friendship would ruin the very friendship they now had.

Peter's diary

There has been a bit of trouble today and violence which I hate to hear. Men behave badly most of the time and are always quick to anger and violence. I was always aware my fellow gardeners had an interesting history and struggled with the violence in their past. But today the man who brings his women to the gardens and pays for people to garden for him while he sits admiring other people's work was assaulted. I heard the sickly thud of a fist on cartilage. I had been sitting among the peas in a sort of meditation. I was practicing my breathing but I was struggling because the rhythms of the evening had been replaced by music. I don't come here to listen to music. I thought that when I lost my sight that I would become a solipsist. The world would be a creation of my own mind and like my allotment I could control what happened. Man, always wants to tame nature and create images of himself in all around him. But the loss of a visual reference in my mind was quickly replaced by a greater heightening of my other senses. Instead of my mind discarding the information and becoming dependent on my vision all changed now I can smell rain coming, I can smell each of my fellow gardeners and can identify them. Freddie always wears a lot of aftershave, I can tell Tom and the vicar from the sound of their walk, I can tell Greggory from the languid way he works always seemingly effortless, while being productive at the same time. My hearing has become so acute that even when I hear the dull sounding voices from within a closed shed talking about strange things like guns, timings, police presence and stolen vehicles it feels as clear as if the people talking were in front of me. These men who are always good and kind to me are hatching all sorts of problems for themselves and it will end badly.

Chapter Eight

After a suitable time and only a knowing wink across the church after Sunday prayer Hans found himself two weeks later walking up the garden path of Mrs Simpson's small but elegant cottage. He noticed the strong smell of a lavender hedge which ran either side of the York Stone path. The front door was bright yellow and had two large fuchsia trees either side of it with the little red flowers adding to the colour of the scene. The cottage was single story and had a thatched roof, a rarity in 1980s Worcestershire. In the windows hung the whitest net curtains Hans had ever seen. In the left-hand window hung a Navajo dream catcher and in the window on the right hung a Greek ornament. Hans was a little surprised that a woman of Christian proprietary would have such pagan symbols in the windows of her home. He thought about asking her this when the door opened before him and Mrs Simpson appeared with a large smile.

Hans had handpicked Peonies wrapped in brown paper and the tin of chocolate powder he had bought from an expensive chocolatier on his last trip to Austria. But Mrs Simpson's heart could not be unlocked by such frivolous gifts as chocolates and flowers. What she wanted more than anything else in the world was company. For loneliness had become the great scourge of modern society. Busy people, too little time for even the basic social interactions and the end of traditional family observances such as regular visiting and sharing meals. Now we entered the age of the lonely people, and that struck hardest at the oldest in society. Mrs Simpson was a lovely person with at times a gushing and overwhelming personality. She was large and she was great fun to be around but she had so few people in her life. The magazine culture of the body-beautiful had torn so many away from the reality of what women actually looked like. Endless diet advice and models stick-thin and beautiful had crushed the worth out of so many women who had equal beauty in the eyes of many. One day the same self-worth, masculinity and body image problems would be delivered on men and see how they jolly well like it she often thought. So, she was nervous to see Hans and was worried that she would not be attractive enough for this particular man. Hans fitted the bill of a pleasant little romance but she knew too that he was a strong and reliable man. A good man, a pillar of the church and if his occasional drifts into serious crime could be dissuaded in the same way that his appalling dress sense could be managed given time. For women love dressing their men as much as they enjoy dressing themselves. She would land a real catch, a man who had the novelty of being from a different country and culture. A man who rejected his past and had studied hard and become a doctor of medicine and, until recently, had practiced in a clinic in Worcester where he was known to be accurate in his diagnosis and also a deft hand at minor surgery. It was such a shame that his wife had died so young and he had managed being a widower for so long. But that was to change, or so she hoped on this glorious early autumn evening.

Hans too was nervous, he had after all been caught red handed committing an armed robbery by a woman he knew from the church and who he had singularly admired. He was often catching glances across the font and he always made a beeline to her cake stall at the church functions. For Mrs Simpson was a stupendous baker with such skill and knowledge that she could make the mouth water just at the thought of her pastry which many people considered the best they had ever eaten. Hans also liked the larger lady, a trait that made him a very attractive proposition to women in almost any town and city the world over. He admired the Victorian nudes in art galleries and he had regarded Marylyn Monroe as too skinny to be a sex symbol much to the consternation of his fellow medical students in the 1950s. Mrs Simpson already had a hold on his imagination plus he knew that she also had a hold on a lengthy prison sentence for them all if she was to talk after all she was a goodly Christian lady. Hans was not here on the doorstep with flowers in hand to protect the Allotment Gang. He was there because he was ready for love and Mrs Simpson was the perfect opportunity to become a man again.

"Good evening, Mrs Simpson."

"Oh, Hans let's not be formal about this. Please call me Loolie."

"Loolie is an interesting name."

"I have been called that since I was a girl. I am really a Mary but my nieces and nephews always called me Loolie and it sort of stuck. Come in. Are they for me? My absolute favourite, Peonies. Did you grow them yourself?"

"But of course."

"There is so much love put into making a gift rather than buying a gift don't you think?" At the word love she blushed heatedly and realised that she may have overstepped the mark so early on.

But Hans was not fazed by this at all; he was in fact aroused, for he could see in Loolie's eyes and the tremor of her lip that the nervousness and desire he felt was being reciprocated nicely. He had not seen endless patients worried and concerned about their condition without being able to read people well. It was a gift like a good bedside manner or playing the flute.

"I will just pop these in a jug of water."

"I brought you a little something from my home in Austria," said Hans.

"What is it?" Loolie asked.

"It is chocolate powder. The finest from my cousins' shop in Hallstatt. He is a master chocolatier and this powder can be used to make the best bedtime gifts in all of Christendom." And now it was Hans's time to blush because the word bedtime gifts were perhaps a little too early. But Mrs Simpson giggled like a teenager and sat next to him on the floral sofa.

"You have green eyes Loolie. Do you know only 2% of humans have green eyes?"

"I think I did. But they are not pure green, they have flecks of brown in them." Loolie shifted herself on the sofa and plumped up one of the cushions and leant into it.

"Beautiful," said Hans.

"Thank you, Hans, you say the sweetest things."

The next few hours were those perfect hours which exist at the start of great friendships. When conversations ranged far and wide across their life's interests and shared hopes for the future. Wine was produced and drunk and then Port which they discovered was a secret pleasure they had both had. No mention of the robbery was made and Loolie laughed at all Hans' jokes and anecdotes and they shared the gossip of the village. Loolie knew some of his story about him being a doctor in a GP surgery. He told her that at the start of the war he had been conscripted into the army and then chosen because of his height and his intelligence to be a paratrooper. This had spared him the worst of the war because special forces had been rarely used. He had parachuted into Crete and had been stationed there for a short while. He had missed the terrible behaviour of the German army towards the people of Crete. He had been captured near Falaise in a wood by the Americans and at the end of the war he was in a prison camp in Stoke Heath, Worcestershire, and had been working on local farms as a labourer. By 1946 he was allowed out without guard and by the end of that year he was to be repatriated. But he did not want to return to his native Austria. His immediate family had been killed in the great bomber raids of 1944 when the American bombed by day and the British by night. He had discovered that he had inherited a bit of money and he used this to pay his way through medical school in Manchester where another more famous paratrooper was to play football for Manchester City. At first it was difficult to get work since the post war prejudices were still apparent. So, he found a medical practice that needed a locum in Worcester and had served there until his retirement. He married a farmer's daughter who sadly passed away before children could be even thought of. It was all so tragic and for a while he thought he was doomed so he, like many men before him and after him, filled his day with work.

Loolie's story was quite different. She had been born at the start of the war. Delivered on the day war broke out and for years her friends and family said that Mr Hitler was destined to lose for she was a formidable woman. She had become a school teacher and had worked hard and married the first man to fall in love with her. She settled to start a family but there was something wrong with one of them and no child came. She regarded this still as one of the great cruelties of life and she became every child's favourite aunt for she was generous with both affection and gifts. She ended her career as a headteacher of a primary school in Droitwich. On her retirement people came from far afield to celebrate her achievement such was the love and respect that she had commanded. Fair but firm she said of herself that is the essence of good teaching and of life. She still got stopped in the village by adults who she had taught years before and she always struggled with names. So, she would say: "ah yes, you have very neat writing."

Suddenly their talk had ended them at the midnight hour and Hans reluctantly made his goodnights. They had a sweet hug at the door and Hans walked down the road home with a spring in his step. Loolie closed the front door and leant back against it and held her heart.

"Love if you are out there, hurry up." She whispered to herself.

Her eyes felt watery and lambent with love. They both knew right there and right then that they were each other's answer. Whatever the question may be. In that hug she had estimated his size and had decided to buy him a nice new sweater to replace the old fashioned one he had arrived in. It was a consummation of sorts, but it was the start of many years of happiness together.

Peter's diary

There is something wonderful about poached eggs on buttered toast. It is a great start to the day. I had slept badly again with vivid dreams and then long periods of reflection in the night hours. Freddie picked me up after breakfast and I went to my allotment and worked. Riding on the back of his Velocette makes me feel slightly nauseous, the journey is quite short but it is all movement and noise. I think this unbalanced me but it is good of him to bring me. The bike would be a total thrill if I could see. But there is no time for self-pity today. Freddie asked me if I had heard anything about the post office robbery. I didn't even know there had been a robbery. He said "Oh!" in a manner that suggested that I was not in tune with the world and then walked off to do his work. I left the spare helmet on the motorbike and set to my chores. I miss teaching and I miss the time spent with inquisitive minds. The interesting questions that they asked and the humour that surrounds young people. But then I like being with these older men and women. Some went to Oxford and others had lived through a time when people wanted to educate themselves rather than just comatose in front of the television or watch endless sport.

I was putting finger posts into the ground today with the help of Rosie. I am quite able to move around without the need to reference points but I had a fall a week ago and Rosie asked if we should put in some wooden posts to enable to locate where I am in the allotment. The first one we put in is next to where Freddie parks his bike and the second and third ones are on turns in and out of the shed and pergola area. Today we put two in at the end of my allotment path. Rosie had turned the ends if the posts so they all felt different at the top. I said I don't really need them but they are good reference points and it was kind of her to help.

Chapter Nine

Two evenings later a full liveried police car in sky blue and white pulled up in the Star Inn car park. Inside were three police men. Two were wearing full uniform and one looked like an unwashed scruffy man who would not look out of place in the back room of a sex shop. They climbed out of the car and walked into the allotments. The officers were looking from side to side, as if they lived their lives constantly in a crime scene or wary of attack. But in the early evening, the Star Inn allotments took on a beauty that sated the soul and made even the weary eye relax. Their big black coppers shoes crunched along the pebble path and onto the brick walkway. The ticky tack of metal studs sounded on the brick work. The officers looked and sounded instantly out of place. The blue uniforms, smart and clean, stood out among the green. They exuded suspicion and distrust, like all men who have spent too long dealing with the worst aspects of life. They walked past the Vicars plot, looked at the little social area, which was empty but for a chess set and a bottle of beer. They continued past Greggory's plot and down to Mr Griffins who was sat in his wicker chair wearing his light pink shorts and pastel blue button-down shirt. They pushed through his gate and appeared to welcome him in a formal manner. Five sets of eyes had lifted from the soil, from hoeing, from digging, from harvesting and followed the procession. This was not a welcome arrival and the beads of sweat that were normally on each brow, now needed more regular attention.

How have they found us, Tom thought? How had they worked it out so quickly? What stupid mistakes have we made? What clues were left behind? Had Mrs Simpson talked?

The questions rattled like a machine gun through his mind as he picked pea pods and placed them into a flat wicker trug.

Mr Griffin produced two chairs from his shed with far more theatricality than would normally be required; it was as if he wanted the world to witness the visit from the police. Savage in uniform sat down with Hunter. The third officer stood at the gate like he was guarding 10 Downing Street. No one could hear the conversation but it seemed jocular and animated from the distance of the Allotment Gang.

"So, you asked for a little show of strength," said Hunter to his brother-in-law. "Looks like someone gave you a fat lip. Which one was it?"

"That doesn't matter now. I just wanted to put the fear of God into them. Thank you for coming. Who are these two?"

"Oh, this is Savage and that one at the gate is Eddington. He's our fingerprint guy. We have just been out doing a bit of work on the robbery."

"What robbery?"

"You must have heard there's been an armed robbery in the last few weeks and we are no nearer catching the buggers as we were when we started. They are clearly a well-run outfit. In and out in a flash. May have even come up from London. A proper professional firm. We checked over our local villains and they all seem squeaky clean. If they could ever be clean that is."

"Any fingerprints?"

"No, they are too good for that. They turned up, did the job and vanish into thin air. But the funny thing is they only got a few thousand quid. So, Savage here thinks they may be just a bunch of kids who are starting out in the game. We have been checking up on the wannabe gangster brigade and as you might guess there's one of those on every estate."

"We think the shooters are fake." said Savage

"If they are kids, they would not get access to guns that easily," Hunter said airily. "This is not your average pissed up villain though. They are good."

"That reminds me I've got a little something for you. Griffin stood up and went to retrieve three good bottles of whiskey which were in a cloth bag. Just a little something for coming."

"Well, we must get going. I hope us turning up can help solve whatever difficulty you have here."

Savage and Hunter stood and shook hands elaborately with Griffin and walked back along the path. Just as they were half way down Savage stopped Hunter with a tug on the arm.

"What is it?"

"Look." Savage had spotted Greggory working the hoe in his patch.

"Let's take a look."

"Alright mate," Hunter said, looking at Greggory. They moved onto his allotment looking at the plants.

"How's it going fella?" Savage said, looking at Greggory with suspicion and then moving around the allotment in the opposite direction to Hunter. The pair suddenly took on the air of big cats sniffing out prey.

Greggory nodded. He had had enough dealings with the police over the years to know that it did not matter if he stayed calm or protested loudly, he would still be searched and turned over. It was just a fact of life.

Hunter looked at the plants, but could not see anything he recognised. He nodded back to Greggory and walked on. But Savage stopped next to a patch of burned soil with new clippings on. He spotted something on the burnt ground. He turned over a piece of wood. Took out a pair of tweezers and lifted out of the embers a piece of charred blue boiler suit.

"Sarge!"

"What is it?" Hunter walked back onto the allotment expecting to see Savage holding up a plant. Greggory continued to hoe as if nothing had happened.

"Look at this." Savage lifted the blue fragment of boiler suit up to the face of Hunter.

"Don't be so fucking ridiculous Savage. When have you ever met a black bank robber? They don't rob banks, they sell drugs. It's the first thing you learn in the police. Come on I want to get home in time to watch the Villa on Match of the Day."

Savage chucked the blue fabric back onto the fire-stained soil, followed his boss out of the allotments and drove off. It would seem that the Allotment Gang were saved by the very racism that brought the police to their door.

Freddie and Tom had watched the scene on Greggory's allotment as it unfolded. They could tell that this was intimidation but they knew Greggory would handle the situation. They wondered if they had been found out but watching the police drinking with Griffin the realisation dawned on them that this was Griffin's way of putting the frighteners on them for Rosie chinning him days before.

Tom walked over to Freddie who was leaning on a hoe and asked if Freddie was thinking the same. They looked over at Griffin who was in his chair again, shirt off and red braces hanging in loops at his side. Griffin raised a glass of whiskey and saluted them. He whispered a mocking toast "Fucking old soldiers."

"Two can play at that game." Tom said. He turned to Freddie. "It's time George got his allotment back. I think we should endanger Mr Griffin and I think I may have an idea."

The next day Mr Smith, a short and balding man in brown overalls, turned up at the church to begin work on the electrical system that had caused the Reverend James such consternation and worry over the summer. Either side of the door two large pots of white flowering Saxifrage quivered like naughty children in the breeze. He knocked at the door of the vicarage to be welcomed by a bleary-eyed vicar.

"Reverend James?" Said Mr Smith removing his cloth cap with a deference he was not accustomed to for he was a forthright and proud man but this was a man of the cloth and he deserved the respect that he was due.

"Here to start work sir. Is it ok to bring the van up to the door? Got quite a bit of kit to get in."

"Sorry, it's Mr Smith, isn't it? You came a month ago to give me a quote. I'm sorry there must be some mistake. We have not raised the money yet to order the work to be started."

"Are you sure sir? I had a letter last Friday telling me to start work today and I have been paid the full amount up front. I have already paid it into my account in cash."

"My oh my. Well, I never," said the vicar wistfully.

*

The following morning, Tom sat opposite Marianne in the Dover Street café. A true greasy spoon café if ever there was one. But they did the best breakfasts in the county and they were cheap. Marco, the owner was a corpulent Italian man with the ability to look dishevelled and dirty in any setting. He wore baggy corduroy trousers with a Hawaiian shirt which stretched out across his formidable belly like a dress. Marco had a round face and his hair ran in dark strands combed over his bald head.

He spoke perfect English in a heavy accent but if he did not like someone he would mutter in Italian under his breath. He always seemed to have a frying spatula in his hand and an off-putting habit of gripping the crotch of his trousers. The café had a lino floor and stainless-steel tables with a centre piece of sugar dispensers and bottles of sauces. Each table had a spoon attached to the table with a light chain. Tea was served in grey mugs, never cups and never saucers.

In one corner sat four young men dressed like extras from a music video. They were writing slogans on banners and whispering in conspiratorial tones. A pile of Socialist Workers Party newspapers sat on the table between them. The door opened, and in stepped another of their group. A tall thin man with a goatee beard. He announced his presence by saying "The smell of death in here is overwhelming" and then slid in next to a hippy-looking girl. At this point Marco shouted back "If you don't like it here sonny you can clear off" while proffering a mug of tea in front of him.

"Meat is murder" came the reply.

"Do you wanna the frickin tea or whaa?" said Marco in his mellifluous Italian English accent.

Marco liked these boys however much grief they gave him because he had been a communist as a young man many years ago. He had left Italy in the 1950s and through trials and tribulations had ended up with this small café in Worcestershire. He retained his thick Italian accent. The little group came in most weekends and wrote out their banners for whatever march they were on that day. Today the banners read 'Coal not Dole' and their newspaper front cover contained the face of Arthur Scargill. They were good regular and entertaining customers, even when they criticised the meaty menu.

"I don't suppose you have any hummus do you Marco?" asked the shortest of the young men wearing an old Royal Navy sailing cap covered in buttons and badges and a 'Frankie says Relax' t shirt. Marco raised his eyebrows.

"I can do you a veggie pizza. But no hummus."

The man with the goatee beard leant in and said to the pretty young woman 'I make my own hummus.'

Tom and Marianne snorted at the same time. Their suppressed giggles had to be fought back when they realised, they were being observed. Tom composed himself and they both settled into a plate of sausage, bacon, eggs, tomatoes, and fried bread.

"A rare treat," said Marianne.

"Me too, but I like it here. Marco is a lovely man. I would come in everyday if my waist line would permit it."

"Oh, you have a great physique for your age," said Marianne.

"I have good news," said Tom

"Really how exciting," purred Marianne in her jolly sing-song voice.

"Yes, the Parish council agreed that the library had to be saved and the Chairman contacted the county councillors. They are all Tories and bloody Masons. Thick as thieves."

"Tom, get to the point," Marianne said testily

"They are going to give you, or rather the Parish Council, the library building for a peppercorn payment of a single penny a year."

"That is marvellous Tom."

"There is no other money with it though. It would be a capital transfer only, so you will need to find the £6000 or two thousand for the first year for it to go through. You will need to set up a trustee's group to manage the concern. They have put a clause in the contract that if the trustees fail to maintain the library the asset would be transferred back to the county council. So, you can't afford to fail. Do you have £2000?"

As soon as Tom asked the question, he knew how he would be able to help further. He thought he could encourage the others to take part in another adventure. It was after all a good cause. The others would not turn down a good cause. Tom was starting to feel alive again after a long time living with grief. He felt better each morning. His day time was no longer less interesting than his night time dreams. When your dream world is more fun than your waking hours then there is something deeply wrong with your life. He felt cheered and he had started to think more about Marianne and less about his wife. The balance was returning to his days. The Post Office raid had energised him, made him feel like a man again and more importantly allowed him to act against the injustices that surrounded him. Each night he watched the police charging into striking miners wielding batons, he watched as the cities burned in riots. The country was going to hell in a handcart and he did not want to sit by and watch. He was going to do something about it all.

"How is your mother?" said Tom, changing the subject.

"Oh, I have had a difficult time with her," Marianne said. "It's getting too embarrassing at times."

"What has happened now?"

"I had taken her some sandwiches yesterday morning to have with her morning tea, You know just little square ones. She likes old fashioned pate, but they tend to give her paste in the nursing home and don't take the crusts off. I know it's horribly vulgar." Marianne gesticulated in a dismissive manner.

"Go on," said Tom.

"Well she announced, after the first bite, to my consternation and shame and in her loud shrill voice that....." Marianne paused for the full effect of the drama to sink in. "She liked a bit of tongue."

Before Tom's brain could warn him not to, he was already grinning.

"She... likes a bit of tongue," Tom repeated.

"I know Tom and that dreadful Bert Smith grinning like the village idiot from ear to ear could not resist making some lewd comment which mummy took in her stride, bless her. He should be locked in his room, the dirty old man."

"Apart from your mother's desires are you well?" said Tom thinking he could have worded the question a bit better, but pleased that he had got away with it when Marianne continued.

"I have been thinking about those poor people in India. Gassed to death by the chemical plant leak. Too awful to contemplate. They won't be helped, will they? We are all just expendable as far as big business is concerned."

"You are starting to sound like a socialist Marianne."

"Don't be ridiculous Tom. By the way, do you know who Frankie is?"

"Frankie? The only Frank I know plays prop forward for the village rugby team down in Finstall Park. Not sure he is known as Frankie though."

"So many young people are wearing these vastly baggy t-shirts with things Frankie has said on them. They are all over the place. Is he a philosopher?"

"Would have to ask Pete about that. I have no idea."

"Well apparently today he wants to both relax and arm the unemployed."

"It's just kids messing Marianne, slogans on t-shirts don't tend to make for revolution. You watch, nothing will change."

"How was the trip to Paris with your sister?" said Tom, sensing the need to change the subject.

"Oh, it was fine except she insisted on taking me to a graveyard to see some dead rock star and the grave of Oscar Wilde. It was covered in red lipstick kisses."

"Doesn't sound that interesting. Was the Eiffel Tower closed?"

"Not at all she said everyone does the Eiffel Tower and the Louvre so we should go and see some graves instead. I would have preferred the Louvre myself. What was most peculiar was that Oscar Wilde's grave has this stone man bent forwards like he's in a gale force wind. Very art deco. And someone had chopped off...mm."

"Yes?"

"Well, someone had hacked off his gentleman bits, with a chisel. I mean who would do such a thing? Where would you keep it?"

"On the mantelpiece?" said Tom.

"Don't be disgusting Tom."

"It would certainly be a talking point at a dinner party," said Tom.

"Not the sort of dinner party I would be seen at. The world has become a place I no longer seem to fit into Tom. Hacking off a, you know what, on a great man's grave seems to be nonsensical. That's all I can say."

In the opposite corner of the cafe sat Rosie with two of her grandchildren. Rosie was dressed in dungarees and a red checked shirt. The children were much smarter as if they had been attending church. The girl was in a red checked dress with white socks and the shiniest of black shoes. The little boy was dressed in a tweed jacket and grey shorts. Tom waved over at them and Rosie waved back.

"Who is that grandma?" said the little girl.

"Oh, that is Tom he is a friend of the vicar and he works with me on the allotments." Rosie said as she bit into a fried egg sandwich.

"He is a friend of the vicar." exclaimed the boy who twisted round to look towards Tom and Marianne.

"Do you believe in God grandma?" said the girl.

"No, I believe in science and maths, my lovely. I guess they are sorts of faith as well."

"How can you not believe in God grandma when mummy takes us to church every week and believes in God?" said the boy.

"That is your mother's choice and one day you will have that choice too."

"So why don't you believe in God grandma?" said the girl while munching on a piece of toast.

"My friend Peter once told me about a mathematician called Blaise Pascal."

"Is he French grandma?" said the girl.

"That doesn't matter. What he said was that if we were not sure that God existed then we should play it safe because when we die the benefits of faith are so huge that it is better to have believed and to have worshipped."

"Is it sort of like making a bet grandma?" said the boy.

"How clever you are Henry" said Rosie "It is called Pascal's wager."

"So, if it is a good bet grandma why don't you believe in God?"

"The problem Henry is which god do you believe in? I believe in kindness. As long as you are always kind you will always be close to God. Maybe kindness is God. Come on eat up your toast I want to take you bowling." Rosie laughed heartily and gave the little girl a tickle.

Tom and Marianne finished their breakfast and after a second mug of Marco's tea and an argument over who was paying, they left the café. Both had enjoyed themselves and both realised that they had more in common than their differences and they liked their differences anyway. Marianne walked off towards the library wearing a floral dress that rose and fell in the breeze. Tom put on his flat cap, pushed his hands in his pockets and watched the orbit of her hips move as she walked away. He smiled. Today was a better day and everyday life was getting better, he thought.

Peter's diary

It is still warm out and the recent heavy rain showers have led to a growing spree. As I walk about, I keep feeling the over grown plants caress my face. The big sunflowers are a little danger because there are often bees on them and I don't want one to brush my face and sting me. Rosie told me today that the police had been to visit the allotments after she had punched Griffin. She said she was both anxious and thrilled to have seen them. But they had not spoken to her. They had talked to Greggory though. But he said that he wasn't intimidated by them and accepted that it would only be him that was spoken too. It wasn't our local bobby who came, who Greggory knows well. These were city coppers he said. Rosie said she would have been happy to have been arrested for assault, she would have made sure that the press would have the full story in required. She has a bit of a martyr complex, I think.

Chapter Ten

The summer turned to autumn and the leaves began to curl up, then become golden as the trees shed them ahead of winter. The sun remained but the air became cooler and then cold. The morning blue sky and chill produced the first frosts and the allotments took on a different hue. The verdant greens of summer became browns as the turned earth dominated the vista. Autumn bonfires filled the air with heavy smoke. A different kind of planting occurred as winter crops went into the soil. Weeding and hoeing paused. Watering was unnecessary. The rains came as drizzles and then torrents. The water butts filled to the top captured from the roof of the Old Star Inn. The sunny mornings became rarer and the blue sky turned to gun metal grey, the clouds sitting low over the earth. There was less work once the fruit trees had been harvested. Across the village jams bubbled in sugar before being placed lovingly into jars. It had been an abundant crop and they would be selling the jams at the church 'bring and buy' well into next summer. Reverend James could put a jar of jam into each food parcel as a small luxury sat among the potatoes, leeks, carrots and cauliflower and courgettes. They would go to the Alms Houses, of which there were ten scattered about the village.

The Allotment Gang got on with their daily duties. A rotavator had been hired and one by one the soil was turned in each of the summer beds. A journey down to old man Henshaw's farm had been made and a trailer or two of horse manure had been brought back, shovelled and wheel barrowed around the site with only the odd grunt and groan of conversation to let us know that the work had become very physical again.

The evening post work socialising had moved inside of Tom's hut where he had a small table and a potbellied wood burning stove. It looked like a room in a prisoner of war camp but for the tools that hung neatly from hooks on the wall. Small red terracotta pots sat in the window with whispers of plants pushing through the soil. A pack of playing cards sat on the table and a kettle steamed on the stove. It was warm after a day spent in the cold.

Tom, Hans, Greggory and Freddie sat around the table. It was poker night. They all wore thick pullovers and hats indoors.

Greggory dealt two cards each and betting consisted of pennies and two pence pieces. The table was littered with copper coins. After the blinds were played three cards were placed up right on the table: the two of clubs, the jack of hearts and five of diamonds.

"Check." said Freddie

"We need to go again," said Tom.

All four men put the cards they were holding back on the table. They looked into Tom's face which remained constrained as if the two Jacks he had been holding were exposed in the worst tell ever.

"Whatever for," said Freddie, "we had a bit of fun, the girl got sorted and the church is safe again and no one got hurt. Even the bloody car was returned."

"Running better than before," added Greggory.

"The library is going to close for want of a few thousand pounds. When we stop reading books, we are no longer a civilisation. My country is losing the fight for civilised life. Cuts to everything, dole queues, strikes, rioting in the cities, pointless wars. Now the books are being taken away."

"What do you mean?" said Freddie

"He who first burns books," muttered Hans.

"The council has given notice that the library will close. We cannot let that happen."

"I'm in," said Freddie self-righteously. "I am not spending my early life shooting down Jerry, no offence Hans."

"None taken," said Hans.

"To be forced to buy books when there is a perfectly acceptable library in the village," he said waving his copy of Huckleberry Finn and slamming it down onto the card table. "Plus, that Marianne is an absolute angel."

"Marianne says that it could be purchased from the council for a peppercorn price and could be run by volunteers, but the running costs will need to be covered by someone. She says six thousand pounds would see it stay open for five years."

"So, you expect us to risk 25 years in jail for another armed robbery to save a library." said Gregory. He grinned.

"Yes," they shouted and clinked their glasses together over the cards.

"Well, I noticed that when the garage on the A36 was turned over last year by those idiots who got caught bragging to their mates on CB radio. They took £3200 on a Sunday night."

"Oh, I remember that. It was in the papers. The judge said they were the most incompetent thieves he had ever had before him. They had told all their mates they had been out on night time "taxation" duties. They had daft names like 'rubber duck', the 'black panther' and such like. They caught two of them because they did not even use code names. The other two were never found."

"Alruyt thees is Muyke Davies just been out and done a garidge." Gregory quipped with a deep Birmingham accent. They all laughed.

The interesting thing is that as petrol has gone up in price, so have the takings of the big petrol companies. This would be a crime without a victim.

"We just march in at 10.30pm on Sunday night and we would take all the money from the weekend. There is CCTV and just one teller on a Sunday. He is barely twenty years old. He will shit himself and hand it all over double quick. We will be in and out in less than a minute. Motorbike round the corner. No need to nick one. We can be back here using the country roads past the Leigh Arms and Queens Head Pub. They will be empty. No traffic anywhere. Back here hide the money, hide the bike, burn the clothes like last time."

"Well, you are not using my Velocette that's for sure. You will have to pinch one," said Freddie.

"I take it you are in then?" Tom smiled.

"I'm in too," said Gregory.

"But first we need to sort out Griffin."

That evening Hans stayed in the allotments until it was dark. He was reading Treasure Island and had reached the point where the ship was being fitted out for the voyage and the crew, ostensibly procured by Long John Silver, were coming aboard. Hans switched down the hurricane lamp and walked out onto the allotments. He did not see Peter who was sitting in the dark waiting for his lift home. Hans walked towards Griffin's hedge and went through the gate into the allotment. He approached the door which was padlocked and chained. Hans produced a thin needle and picked the lock. It took him three minutes and he was cross with himself for taking so long. Hans closed the door behind him and switched on his torch. He scanned the torch around the interior. The chairs and table were stacked behind the door. There was a sink against the wall and a cabinet with all sorts of drinks in. There was a fridge and a large bed. Hans picked up one of the chairs and stood it in the comer opposite the bed. He climbed onto it and taking a small camera from his pocket he placed it in a spot on a beam running across the roof. He angled it carefully. Stepped down and went and lay on the bed. He could see the lens. But only when he shone the torch directly onto it. He got off the bed, flattened the sheet, put the chair back on the table and came out of the shed, closing the door and securing the lock. It was harder to lock the padlock than it had been to open it. He walked out of Griffin's allotment and back down to his car.

*

A few days later Greggory's son turned up at the allotment. Bernie was a big man which was odd because Greggory was small and wiry like a bantam boxer. He came to tell his father what his father didn't want to hear, that he was in a bit of bother. Bernie worked the doors in Birmingham and had been borrowing money to play in a big stakes card game. For much of the time he did well and he thought that he could make a living out of gambling rather than talking down drunks from nightclub doors. Bernie had trained as a surveyor and had been quite successful at it, but he found the work dull. He had two children of his own who he doted on and looked after in the day while his wife worked as a midwife. The shift work suited both of them and allowed them to handle the child care successfully. Bernie was able to pick them up from school and cook their dinner while waiting for his wife to get home. They would then pass in the hallway and she would always say: "Get with the programme Bernie."

Gregory looked up from his squashes and saw Bernie walking down the path towards him smiling.

"Alright dad, how are you?" said Bernie.

"How much did you lose?" Gregory said, looking down and pulling out clumps of weeds.

"How did you know?" Bernie looked crestfallen.

"I always know. It's written all over your face."

"It's a bit worse than that dad. Have you heard of a man called Reg Wheeler?"

"No, who is he?"

"He is a big shot gangster and I owe him two grand. Except he doesn't want me to pay back the money, just do him some favours, odd jobs, deliveries you know."

"I can guess Bernie. Is he a bad man?"

"As bad as they get dad." Bernie picked up a hoe and started to run it through the soil.

"Your mother and I didn't bring you up to end up in trouble all the time."

"I'm not in trouble all the time. I just got unlucky. It's the last time I will ask dad I promise."

"Try and hold him off for a bit. I will see what I can do. When does he need the money?"

"He doesn't dad, that's what I am saying. I am waiting for him to ask me a favour or give me a job."

"Well, that is going to get you into trouble isn't it. We had better find the money. Pass me the hoe. Have you been to see your mother?"

"Every week dad."

"How is she doing?"

"She is doing just fine."

"Good, now pass me that green twine and let me think how we can solve your little problem."

Greggory watched as his son worked the twine delicately to surround the tomatoes as they rose up the bamboo poles. He was pinching the plants out as he worked. Greggory was not thinking how he could solve the issue of the debt but was remembering years ago standing at the bottom of the allotment on the banks of the little brook that flowed with some vigour round the meandering bends. He could see Bernie with a fishing net dipping it excitedly into the fast-flowing water with Rosie holding him round the waist to stop him from falling in. Bernie was wiggling and Rosie was saying not to wriggle or he'd fall in and the sharks would get him.

Later Greggory went to see Rosie. He always turned to Rosie when he had a problem. Rosie was good at listening and giving advice but rarely asked it for herself. He resented that she never asked him for advice but it did not stop him from asking her. They sat facing each other on old leather arm chairs that Rosie had rescued from the local tip. They had a mug of tea each. Rosie, even sitting down, towered over Greggory.

Rosie was enjoying a cheese and pickle sandwich and was tearing big chunks of bread into her mouth and chewing noisily.

"Do you know what Gregory? I am always hungry. I think it is all the fresh air and work here in the allotments. I am worried that I am getting a sun tan from my fridge light. I'm visiting it so often." she quipped. Rosie slurped her tea and took another enormous bite out of the sandwich.

"Bernie is in trouble again. This time quite big trouble and the potential for it to get a lot worse" said Greggory looking a little crestfallen.

"What has he done now?" asked Rosie through a mouth of butter, bread and cheese.

"It's not so much what he has done as what he will be asked to do." said Greggory.

Rosie swallowed and said "Can you solve this problem for him?"

"I sort of think I can," said Greggory.

He leant back in his chair and sighed loudly. Rosie knew more about human nature than most and realised that she would not get much more out of Greggory until he was ready. She too lent back knowing that Greggory would tell her but only when it felt right for him to do so. Meanwhile she asked him about his roses and was the owner of the mini happy with the turbocharger she had Greggory fit for them.

Peter's diary

I could hear them playing cards. I am never invited to play for good reason, though Rosie said she could create a set of cards that I could feel to find out what I had in my hand. But I am not a gambling man and the others would tire of telling me what cards went down in the flop. Autumn has come and the wind has risen making it difficult for me to hear voices and get around the allotment. So, I work in silence just the sound of the trowel and shovel. I feel my way around the plants and only occasionally ask for help to ensure I am not digging up the wrong thing. Most of my vegetable planting is big stuff and easy to identify sprouts, cabbage, potatoes, tomatoes, green beans, carrots. All easy to plant grow and harvest without too much nurturing. In my shed all the tools have an exact place and I am careful to return each to that exact place after use. Tom had fitted mounts to my shed walls and around the potting table so I can have everything I need in reach. My day was dull. Just a haircut at Billy's and a visit to see Marianne at the library. Hardly worth writing any of this down really.

Chapter Eleven

Alvechurch garage sat on the A36 just off the M5 junction south of Birmingham. It was the flagship garage in a chain of garages across the Midlands. Alvechurch turned over an enormous amount of fuel since it was marginally cheaper than the garages that actually sat on the motorway itself. Trucking firms used it as a cost cutter and the HGV drivers received free coffee and food with each refill. And the coffee was particularly good and the sandwiches were heavy with meat. This meant that the garage made thousands of pounds each day. After the robbery two years before the management had fitted a safe into the upstairs office because after the closure of banking on a Friday afternoon to opening again on the Monday morning the garage was stocked up with cash notes. The company sent its own security to pick up the cash on a Monday morning. Two large thick set men called Barry and Bob would arrive wearing all black combat style uniforms and crash helmets. Few other security arrangements were in place.

Stan Cooper was the manager and he was hard working and reliable. He had a different assistant most days but Stan was in the garage every day and often until quite late. On Sunday he was joined by David Wood a ginger headed punk rock bass player with the local band the Klingons. David was an intelligent twenty-year-old whose dream of university had been squashed with the grades he received for his A levels. He had achieved three Fs and an O. The disappointment of not going to university was only met with further derision from his friends when his grade certificate read F, O, F, F. He would later write a thrashing guitar song about it which no one but his annoyed neighbours ever heard. Bill, as his friends called him, had got this job selling fuel on weekends and working reclaiming bricks from derelict factory sites during the week. In his limited spare time, he rehearsed in the hall of a local primary school with his band and played the occasional small gig in pubs around Worcester and Malvern. David was perpetually crushed by his unachievable life ambition to be a rock star and by his firm belief that he was an intellectual and a natural philosopher and therefore better than anyone else. On Sundays he worked from 2pm until 11pm alongside his boss Stan. Stan was the only person to call him David even his mother and father called him Bill. Stan had no ambition in life and the petrol selling business was perfect for him. He was warm, he got to talk to lots of people and he was paid well in the process. He had a nice semi-detached house on a council estate in Worcester which he shared with his wife and two angry and unhappy children. Stan's wife was no longer in love with him and she used sex as a weapon in their marriage. She told her friends she had not had sex with him for two years. Those friends in turn had told their husbands and those husbands in turn had decided that Stan's wife was worth a visit. Stan worked hard and long hours but on a Sunday evening between 10pm and closing at 11pm he would squirrel himself away in the upstairs office with a few magazines from the top shelf in the garage. He told Bill he was banking which was a close enough approximation. This would leave Bill in sole charge of the garage forecourts which were often quiet at this time. Bill felt relieved when this occurred for Stan had little conversation but for a set of prejudices against the world in general that he considered to be a political belief system. In fact, Stan never voted and had little interest in politics, art, books, films, music or current affairs. This made life difficult for Bill because he liked to talk and talk about everything. He was searching all the time for slogans and lyrics and thought that conversation was a means to clear his own thoughts and ideas and bring them to clarity. He had started to follow the post punk group Crass and had even visited Dial House the punk/hippy commune that they had set up in Essex. He liked the notion that you are in charge of your own behaviour and you should not take orders or follow other people's rules. This was all well and good but he was saving for a Fender Precision bass guitar and they did not come cheap and so he followed orders and engaged in the capitalist system that he would rage against in his personal time.

Bill had just served a driver of a large HGV who had come into the shop soaked from the rain which fell heavily and was writing down a pearl of wisdom from that man who had said "It's National shite day" during a brief conversation about getting home to Bristol before 1am. As the lorry pulled off the forecourt it was throwing it down with rain which was bouncing off the concrete forecourt. The car turned into the t junction off the main A36 and pulled up next to a row of houses with small hedged gardens. The doors opened but no internal light came on in the car. Three men got out and one remained in the driver's seat. All three men were wearing identical blue overalls, bin men coats, balaclavas and stockings over their heads. All three took a quick look around and then trudged towards the garage shop door. One was carrying a large machete, and another had a service pistol stuffed into his jacket pocket.

Tom, Hans and Freddie took a big anxious breath and pushed the door open and charged into the shop.

'Fuck, here we go again,' Bill thought as three thick set men ran towards him one carrying a machete and the other pointing what looked like a gun from a cowboy film straight at this head. Bill stuck his hands instinctively in the air and in doing so missed the opportunity to hit the panic button which would have informed Stan upstairs that they were being robbed.

"All the money in the bag and open the door" said the first man in a decidedly posh accent.

Bill started to stuff the money from the two tills into the bag and pressed the electronic button that opened the windowed door into the controlled area. While the gunman continued to fix the pistol at him the two other men pushed through the security door and ran up the stairs to the office. They entered the office just as Stan was trying to stuff his erect penis back into his trousers. This moment of indignity lost him valuable time to close the safe which was wide open behind the desk. The man with the machete shouted

"Stay away from the safe or I will cut your knob off with this machete." Hans was already in the safe filling a sack with the cash notes.

"Leave the coins," said Tom.

Tom pulled the telephone cable from the wall and he and Hans crashed back down the stairs. The noise of them coming down the stairs startled Bill and he was on the verge of wetting his pants when suddenly they had all gone. One minute he was in danger of losing his life the next silence.

"Stan are you alright? Stan?" he called up the stairs.

Stan was in the process of removing the CCTV video tape and slipping it into his jacket pocket. Something he often did on a Sunday night less someone should view what he was up to. He would have some explaining to do that there was no video in the machine but then the thought of the media getting hold of the story where he was caught masturbating during a robbery was more than he could bear to stand. He put in a blank VHS cassette.

"I'm ok". He replied weakly.

Bill came up the stairs to the office and his first reaction was to pick up the phone.

'Shall I call the police?'

"It's no good they tore it from the wall. Get in your car and drive into Bromsgrove. There's a telephone box just opposite the Woolworths on the way in. I will wait here."

"I think they got it all. The safe was open and I was counting up for the night when they burst in."

Outside the three men bundled themselves into the car and Greggory drove off steadily and without any sense of urgency or panic.

They stayed in their masks and uniforms sitting silently until 20 minutes later they pulled up at the Star Inn car park where they parked the car in the garage and proceeded to destroy all the clothing, masks, gloves and even boots. Greggory began to disinfect all the car surfaces until Hans said to him "No we will burn this one, leave it to me."

Hans got into the car and drove it off. An hour later it was burning brightly outside a disused wrecking yard in Yardley. No one had seen him come or go. He had set the vehicle alight and disappeared into the smoke. He had crossed waste ground to the rear of the yard and met Freddie on the Velocette quarter of a mile away on a side road in a different industrial estate. Meanwhile Tom and Greggory burned the clothing at the allotment. The money was counted and placed under the floorboards in a specially designed chamber they had created out of an old tea chest lined and water proofed. This was lowered down a five-foot-deep hole. It would stay there for only a few days. A false top filled with water was lowered down onto it so should anyone find the hole they would presume it was filled with water and look no further. Hans had said this is how they hid escape equipment in the POW camp he was detained in.

By 2am they were all back together to drink a rum in the allotments. Tin mugs were tapped together in a toast to the success of the raid and a few old soldiers' stories were told. The adrenalin did not leave them as they went their own ways home to their beds.

The next day Tom was at his allotment early. His patch was the least attractive of all of the allotments at the Star Inn. He had neglected it and like him it was only just recovering from the death of his wife. The others had volunteered to help him get things back in shape but James had arrived one day and stopped all work on Tom's allotment. He told them that Tom would be back eventually and they should not interfere. When he was ready again the physical work would give him a return in purpose and peace. James was right, 12 months of neglect, weeds and untilled earth gave way to rigorous activity and a rebirth of the plot. There was still a lot to do. A section of grass lawn that Freddie had put in in his absence remained. Freddie claimed that he needed to grow this so that he could lift it later to replace his small front lawn. On this grass section Monty, the dog lazed with a pink ball between his front paws, almost daring one of the gardeners to pick it up. Tom, wearing brown corduroy trousers, a grey shirt and a green jumper was bent over a rake. He scratched at the earth lost in his thoughts. What if someone had put up a struggle and wanted to be a hero? He thought. We would be in serious trouble if a young man or even a strong young woman refused to comply or worse, grabbed at a mask. This would end this whole game. Tom was the sort of man who over-thought everything. He would extrapolate every part of the plan and filled his nights in bed with what ifs? Invariably these thoughts ended with someone getting hurt. Doubt was a big part of his life. He had doubted his abilities as a soldier during the war, always thinking would he fight or surrender when the time came. He had doubts about the people in his life and it was this that gave him his faith in which he had no doubts. Tom raked at the grass taking out the moss which clogged up the teeth of the rake. He stood it on end and pulled the moss with his fingers. Hans had said to him that nothing had gone wrong, everything went to plan. It was human nature to comply with loud barking orders. By the time people started thinking about being a hero the gang would be gone. It had all been a bit of excitement Freddie had argued when Tom talked about his worries. But he agreed maybe it had all gone a bit too far. No one had been hurt. At the end of it all good things would come from the right people getting the money for a change. Tom returned to his raking and his worrying. He liked the thrill of it all and was embarrassed by this and he knew that redistributing wealth was a pillar of his own personal politics. Why should he worry so much? He sniffed the air and the strong smell of wet grass that reminded him of his father carrying him from the caravan to the toilet block on the summer holidays as a child.

His own father had been a strict disciplinarian and a very devout man in the high church tradition. He would be turning in his grave at the thought of his boy being an armed robber. Tom set these thoughts aside and worked on enjoying the feeling of his muscles working the earth.

Peter's diary

I have always found Hans very mysterious and enigmatic. We talk at the allotments but he is mostly the strong silent type and I can't usually get much conversation out of him other than the odd Teutonic announcement such as "Winter is coming" or "Weather for the dead". He has lately changed the sound of his voice. He sounds more American and I am told by Billy the barber, that he has started a romance with Loolie Simpson in the village. Tonight, I was sat in the snug in the Grasshopper Pub nursing a pint of Banks's mild and listening to the sound of darts striking the dart board and over walked Hans with his beer and joined me for an hour. He was quite chatty in a way I had never experienced before. We talked of the allotments and my medicinal herbs. I suggested a few things for his rheumatism, but as a medical doctor he was a little too dismissive of my suggestions. He talked of being a general practitioner and how he had to listen daily to people's woes for his living. He said it could be a most depressing experience at times and that he knew several doctors who had committed suicide. He was glad to retire and enjoyed his time at the allotment. I knew I was being impertinent when I asked him about his time in the German army something I believe he only ever talks to Tom about. He said he was actually Austrian and when Austria had voted to join Germany in the Anschluss, he became eligible for the army. He said he was very arrogant and vain in those days and had not wanted to be any ordinary soldier and had been selected to be a parachutist. He said he didn't care much for politics but he did say the whole 'Nazi thing', as he described it, had overwhelmed many young people including himself and he had been under its spell as a young man. It was a part of his life he didn't care to remember. "When the evidence changes, we are allowed to change our minds" he said. He had taken part in the invasion of Crete and had been wounded in the jump and had been sent back to Austria to convalesce from a badly broken leg. A bullet had passed through his leg and he nearly bled to death. It meant he had not been involved in the terrible atrocities and war crimes perpetrated against the people of Crete. Later he heard the stories from the soldiers he served with. "I realised then that I was on the wrong side of history". He had been captured by the British and interrogated and had been imprisoned in the camp near Stoke Heath. After the war had ended up in Manchester and had learned to be a doctor. I am sure he left out a lot of detail, some of which he is ashamed of, but I am glad we had the chance to talk. After an hour he left saying he had a date with a wonderful woman. Rosie had said he had been seeing one of the ladies in the village. Winter is indeed coming.

Chapter Twelve

Winter had arrived and so had the frosts. The rhythms of work had changed from the autumn. There was little green in the allotments. Only the evergreen trees had not noticed the change in temperature, while all the deciduous trees had shed their leaves long ago and now stood dark, drawing spiky shapes against the heavy grey clouded sky. Hans's chalked list contained crosses and ticks. Tom had re-felted the roof of two of the sheds. He had hammered away for a week. A bad roof leak had ruined a few of Freddie's records, warping the card covers and dampening the old record player which was out of action for a week, until Rosie fixed it. In early winter the crops had been ready and had been harvested. They had brought in carrots and parsnips, cabbage, maincrop potatoes, late season apples and pears, pumpkins, squashes, beans, onions, shallots, garlic and root vegetables. Peter and Rosie had spent a week wrapping late apples in old newspapers.

The apples and pear trees had been pruned back and chillies and sweet peas had already been sown. Tools had been ground sharp on an old hand grinder. The hedges by the woods had been cut back and folded over between interlaced batons of wood. This was a job they had all worked on together and had taken two days of swearing, cuts and stings and quite a lot of laughter at each other's expense.

Seeds had been ordered and strawberry runners had been potted up. Peter enjoyed the potting the most. The garden areas were mostly open grass, less soil for the job of weeding which was a constant in their lives. On the chalkboard written in capital letters was CLEAN THE POLLY TUNNELS and it was this job that Tom was doing on a crisp cold winter morning. He wore a black donkey jacket, a balaclava which emitted a fog from his breathing and the sweat that covered his head and hair. Tom wore three pairs of gloves, the outer ones being marigold rubber gloves. He felt the cold more in his hands than he had ever done in his life. Only Hans and Tom were working that January winter morning. Greggory's allotment was already pristine, neat and spring ready. It was too early in the day for Peter to be working and Freddie was off at a motorbike show in Shropshire. Hans was also cleaning, but his work was on old plant pots and seedling trays. The occasional car drove along the road breaking the silence and the sounds of crows in the woods. Their raucous cawing the only sound in the freezing air. The cold was so intense that winter that faces burned red after an hour and on one day it was so cold that it was uncomfortable to breathe in the air. There had been a period that winter when the number of jobs had felt overwhelming but they cracked on as industrious as ever, only stopping for a pot of sweet tea. They did not share the time after work together and apart from visits to the church they had seen little of each other. But like all friends any time apart is inconsequential, conversations stopped a week before were carried on as if there had not been a gap of six days.

After the raid on the petrol station, they had decided to get on with life as normal. Not to discuss the £9000 in cash hidden beneath the floor in the potting shed. They only knew it was £9000 because this had made the news. The papers had shrilled in headlines about police incompetence at not finding this gang.

The police had not made any link between the two robberies. The crimes were indeed quite different. There was no CCTV this time so the size of the men could not be compared. There was now a burnt-out car while the first car had been returned.

There was no connection between the returned car and the first robbery because no one knew what it had been used for and why it reappeared. It was presumed the joy riders had simply returned the car. Mrs Simpson had been good to her word and had not said a thing. Stan was circumspect on why there was no VHS in the machine that night and Bill had little to say other than there were three big men dressed in overalls with faces disguised. His enduring memory was the terror of having the cowboy gun stuck in his face and the somewhat posh and calm voice of the gunman.

Savage and Hunter had nothing to go on and had not made a single connection between the two robberies.

Hunter toyed with the idea that it was an out of area job. He thought the posh voice was probably someone from the south. The boiler suits were potentially interesting, as were the balaclavas and stockings, but that was standard fare for modern gangsters to wear. Chasing up boiler suit sales in the industrial West Midlands would be a thankless task and one neither detective wanted to engage in.

"All the clothes are readily purchased and disposable," said Hunter, "we will never see any of the kit again".

The detectives sat in their office, a large open plan room with twenty or more desks and the constant noise of ringing telephones. The office smelled of stale cigarettes and sweat. Various uniformed officers worked telephones and typewriters each sat hunched over desks with half-drunk mugs of tea and folded red topped newspapers. The sergeant at the nearest desk had his newspaper open showing the breasts of a women who was the same age as his youngest teenage daughter. Along one wall were three offices with open doors for the senior policemen. They were all empty. A solitary police woman was walking through the room with three mugs of tea gripped by the handles in each hand. Across the room two officers laughed loudly at a cartoon in the newspaper. On the wall next to Hunter's desk there was a pin board with bits of paper and photographs on it. Descriptions of vehicles, a photo fit drawing of a man whose face was behind a mask.

"Fucking useless that is," Hunter had said, when he had been offered it by the artist who had interviewed one of the witnesses the day before. The phones rang for ages, as worried people wanted to get through to the police. The telephones rang constantly and were left unanswered.

"I can't hear myself bloody think in here" Hunter said with a little menace in his voice.

"What about the cowboy gun Boss?" Savage asked.

"I suspect that it was fake. Who uses cowboy guns?"

"It was probably a revolver of some sort or a starter pistol," said Savage.

"We used to get a few service revolvers in the 60s. Brought back after the war as souvenirs and then sold on. It could have been a service revolver. But the army wised up to weapon storage years ago. You have to check everything in and out now and the records are meticulous. It's more likely to be a toy gun."

"Well, it put the shit up the pair of them so it must have looked real." Savage replied.

Hunter was stuck. The boss had been on to him saying he had two unsolved serious robberies on his books and the press were on his back. "Heads will roll Sergeant if we don't get some progress soon."

Their first link came a few days later when someone reported to Savage that a bloke had been into the station at Borsall Heath saying he had heard CB radio chatter from someone called Big

Reg talking about a little night time shopping off the A36 on Sunday night, that had proved to be profitable.

When Savage told Hunter this, Hunter had turned his head and, smiling said" "They would not be that stupid again surely".

"What do you mean boss?" said Savage.

"I nicked a gang of retards two years ago for doing the same petrol station, well a series of petrol stations and we caught them because they were bragging on CB radio. Two of them were caught and they are doing 8 years each in Wandsworth. The one called big Reg we never got. They would not grass anyone up even when we laid it on thick in the interview." Hunter paused. He shook his head from side to side.

"No one would be that stupid."

"They are a proper firm, these boys" Savage said, "Must be proper tough guys for the other two not to squeal." said Savage.

"Surely it's not Big Reg. He is not that thick. We dismissed him from the investigation last time because he is a proper gangster and proper criminals don't get caught. He is good at being a criminal. He's a proper big time Charlie robbing petrol stations would not give him enough cash. He runs all the doors in Birmingham. Nine grand would be nothing to him. He doesn't make mistakes. He is a big lad as well; he was pulled over for speeding once and it took five coppers to get the fucker in the van after he broke the nose of some probationary new boy." Hunter rubbed his chin. A telephone went off on the next desk and gloom descended across his round face. He scratched at his sideburns making a rasping noise that Savage could hear across the table. "It's not his style. No, it's not him. It can't be."

"Could he be doing it for the sport? You know the sheer thrill of the game of it all. Maybe he's bored" Savage offered.

"That is not a bad idea. But he is a man who enjoys violence. If it was sport, he wanted he would have roughed up the two cashiers. He's the sort of bloke who likes to hear people beg for mercy."

"Could the cashiers be in on it? One of them was the lad who was there last time." said Hunter.

"I looked into them both, boss. The lad plays in some punk band and when I interviewed him, he was quite shaken by the robbery. A bit of a soft lad in my opinion. The other fella was brought in as the manager after the last robbery two years ago. He has no record of anything. Possibly the most nondescript bloke I have ever met. Pretty sure it's neither of them involved. They just look like victims."

"Can we trace the CB traffic? We got the last two clowns with some army triangulation device that CID from London lent us. As soon as they went on air, we had them. Absolute retards. We could not believe our luck. They had been robbing petrol stations for about six months. See if you can get us the kit again Savage," said Hunter.

"Should we go pay Big Reg a visit boss?"

"Not sure I want to wind him up."

"What about the gun?"

"Well, there is a link there because one of the ones we caught was using a starter pistol. His dad was something in local athletics."

"So, it could be a starter pistol?"

"Or a service revolver maybe."

*

Her majesty's government had forgotten, or simply ignored, the merchant seamen who had braved both the Atlantic convoys and the Convoys up to Murmansk through the arctic seas. There were no merchant sailors' medals. An omission that balks with a generation of men who braved the wickedness of the Atlantic storms and ran the gauntlet of the wolf packs and the freezing temperatures of the arctic. Greggory Alambu did hold a medal. He had the highest award for bravery of a civilian and he won it saving the lives of six crew mates pulling them out of an oil drenched sea into a lifeboat he had launched from a ship against the wishes of a commander who wanted to press the ship on to safety under the Sunderland bomber screen. For three days Greggory had nursed the injured men and rowed west until being picked up by a RN corvette out of Liverpool. Greggory, like many other Jamaicans and West Indians, had joined the merchant fleet at the start of the war and had survived what the U boat commanders called 'the happy time'. After 1942 things got better. He had started as an ordinary hand but had quickly become a radio operator and signalman. He gave up the sea in the late 1940s having served on too many ships names to mention. He rarely wore his George Cross but on November 11th he could be seen weeping at the local cenotaph for all his comrades he had lost. Few of the younger generation could recognise a George Cross from all the other medals on display from the elderly men and women of the village. But the men who surrounded him on that day knew who he was and what he had done. What the people of the village did not know nor did the Allotment Gang was that Greggory was working to save his son from having to get dragged into gangland Birmingham and spending time in jail. For Bernie would never make a clever and successful criminal. He was the sort of criminal that got caught. Greggory had set up a receiver and an antenna in a hedge one road away from the home of the notorious Birmingham gangster who Bernie owed money too. Then from his own home 15 miles away in the countryside he selected a CB radio frequency and began to talk to the youth of Solihull under the CB handle of Big Reg. He spoke of taxing the rich and spreading love to the poor he talked to various local people making many cryptic comments. He broadcast for over an hour mixing in conversations about football, boxing and the state of the country.

Less than 100m away from a large mock Tudor mansion equally mockingly named the House of Pain emitted a CB conversation that the police listened to on a recording made by Harry Pratchett an amateur radio operator and CB enthusiast. Mr Pratchett was CB radio enthusiast who annoyed all his neighbours by the number of aerials that came of the roof of his house. His occasional conversations with people as far away as Australia sometimes appeared on his neighbour's television screens. Usually in the middle of some soap opera like Coronation Street or Crossroads. Once Benny from Crossroads started speaking in an Australian accent his next-door neighbours became very agitated. Pratchett had turned up at the police station with a taped conversation from the CB channel and the desk officer had rung Savage and he had been brought up to the central police station in a van. Pratchett felt very grand riding in the police van.

He had gone to an interview room and had produced his reel-to-reel tape recorder to play the conversation to Savage. Afterwards Wheeler had been brought in with a secretary who typed the conversation verbatim.

"Listen to him bragging boss," said Savage

"Breaker, breaker this is Charlie Farley do you copy big man?"

What no one knew in the police station that day was that Big Reg was the call sign of a different man all together and he was fast asleep at the time of the transmission. He had been part of the original petrol station gang but had not used his CB radio since his two friends had been caught. The police also did not know that the real Big Reg did own a CB radio which he had bought for his son as a Christmas present. His spoiled son, who attended an expensive public school, had never used the radio set and so it had remained in a box in the attic of the House of Pain. Finally, Savage, Hunter, the two big Reg's, the secretary and Mr Pratchett did not know that the Big Reg they were listening to was in fact Greggory but what Greggory did know was that Big Reg was a big time Birmingham gangster. Charlie Farley was a small balding twenty something with no actual friends outside of the CB radio world. He lived alone with his mother and worked for the DHSS processing unemployment claims.

"Yes, I copy," said Greggory.

"It doesn't sound like him. I have heard him talk. We had recordings of this two years ago. I have met him and his voice is not that deep. He is surprisingly squeaky sounding for a large man."

"Could just be a cheap CB set boss," retorted Savage.

"How is life treating you Big Reg?"

"Great been out taxing the rich to give to the poor." Big Reg's voice boomed deeply from the small speaker.

Savage looked at his Boss and smiled.

"A nice little earner?"

"Always. The price of petrol is going up though". Big Reg laughed.

"Was that in the Birmingham Mail? I didn't read that."

"This is Big Reg. Naah it's the price you have to pay for my night time deeds."

"This Charlie Farley, say again."

"This is big Reg you owe me money over."

"Sorry buddy over"

"Yeah, you owe me money over."

"I don't know what you are talking about over." Charlie Farley suddenly had an edge of fear in his voice.

"Now listen you cunt. I want it by the weekend or you're a dead man, over." Greggory could barely suppress a giggle.

"Big Reg, this is Charlie Farley we are not allowed to swear on CB radio."

"Just get me the money."

"Any more", Hunter asked.

"Yes boss."

"Play it," Hunter ordered.

"Breaker - breaker, this is Big Reg do you copy?"

"Alright big Reg, this is Carwash over.".

"Alright Carwash how's it going? Have got anything for me?"

"Nothing I can talk about across the radio, Big Reg."

"Ok, Carwash pop into the chew and choke on Monday. This is big Reg out."

"No use that bit, play the one with Charley Farley." Hunter said. They listened to the recording again. He wouldn't be that stupid."

"He may think it's private, boss because once you meet on this system you move to a different band so you can talk. He might think that this made it a private conversation like on a telephone. He may not realise that other people could move to that channel too and listen in," Savage explained.

"Mmmm! I still don't think he would be that stupid." Hunter rubbed his chin.

Savage replied: "It fits though boss. Maybe I was right, he does it for the thrill of the crime. Once a gangster always a gangster."

"There's not enough here for us. Let's put a watch on him and see if there's any sort of money drop or take a look at his spending. Tap his phone too. If he is stupid enough to advertise on a radio system, he will make other mistakes as well. Good work Savage."

*

The House of Pain was the home of Reg Wheeler. He was well known to the people of Birmingham. He was often photographed with show business stars and glamorous women normally coming out of one the city centre clubs. He was perceived by many in the media as a lovable rogue. But he was far from that. The House of Pain was not called this for any other reason than instilling fear in his own employees, his gangland connections and his enemies. Big Reg was a man who enjoyed violence. He enjoyed the sound and smell of violence and he liked instilling fear in everyone who surrounded him. He loved no one and no one would ever love him. He was rarely caught doing anything. However, his list of crimes was long. He would have been in prison for several times the length of his life. He was not just a criminal he was a menace to society at almost every level. You could not do business with him in any form without the fear of violence dictating your behaviour and your prices. You always lost and Big Reg always won. It was a simple fact of Birmingham life. He was loathed as much as he was feared.

Peter's diary

Bitterly cold and morning frosts. The earth smells quite different when it is frozen. It has less vigour and even the smell sends a chill into me. By mid-afternoon everyone was sitting around under the bare pergola in the centre of the allotments. Weary of tidying up jobs and the cold. I missed the summer scents climbing wistfully up the wooden supports of the pergola. Tom has a good nose for planting. Just here, at this table, only a few months ago the smells of Wisteria, Jasmin and Sweet pea. No flowers now and I could smell a burning brazier and pipe smoke. All sat in silence. Then Greggory asked me to produce my magic box. "A special tea moment on a cold day Peter?" He asked. "A little wabi sabi is needed," he added. Everyone needs rituals in life as much as they do routines. It is the routines that keep us focused and makes the good things in life seem so much better. Western Philosophy has been heavily influenced by the ideas from the east and no more so than from Rikyu. Rosie fetched the box from my shed and I began to unpack what is important in life. Old cups with cracks and character are important. Over the years I have compiled a collection of them. One by one I took them from the box. Some have patterns on, Chinese and Japanese ink drawings. My favourite was a Hokusai drawing. I felt for it finding its chipped base and the crack running from the base of the handle. I put this in front of me and the others to its right in a line. Next the old Tranger stove which I assembled and lit with a flint and bar. The sparks I knew were flying into the gas and erupting in a satisfying manner. I told them that in Zen thinking that nothing was lasting and nothing could be perfect, all was impermanent, imperfect and incomplete. Such objects for tea should reflect the notion of humbleness. I could tell they were all watching me now, a pipe had been put on the table and so was a newspaper. I filled the kettle with water from a plastic bottle and placed it on the burner. I turned down the flame to ensure that it would come to the boil slowly. Deferring satisfaction was necessary. As I worked I explained to them again the meaning of wa , kei and Jaku. How important it is to be outside in nature doing this. I opened the tin caddy and measured green tea into each cup. I could feel their concentration as I poured the water into the cups. I asked them to enjoy as I passed each steaming cup to each of them. Silence prevailed for five exquisite minutes. What is sin? Tom asked me today. A strange thing to ask. I tried my best to give him the definition from the religious angle. I think that this made him feel more anxious and agitated and the tranquillity of a simple tea ceremony was now lost as he worked through his thoughts. Hans had stood up as Tom had asked his question and said that he had seen enough sin for one lifetime and he went back to his allotment. I presume he had been a Nazi at some point. I have never discussed it with him.

Tom began to recount in a slow quiet voice. A voice that seemed not his own. He was looking inward at himself as he spoke. We were split up in the chaos. Operation White City they called it. The brass that is. We had entered a village late afternoon early evening. I was so tired and the sweat just poured off me. My uniform was stuck to my body and the slouch hat brim was greasy and salty. All seemed quiet but they were in slit trenches at the edge of the clearing, and we heard the woosh of incoming mortars then the crump sound as they exploded around us. The machine guns opened up and we simply panicked and ran. Ran for my life. Ran like I'd never run before. Could have got the four-minute mile if I'd been timed. After a while I realised that the rest of the platoon were not with me and it was getting quickly dark. So I found a bit of thick jungle and inside there was a hollow in the ground.

I lay down in it and covered myself with leaves and spent the next two nights there while around me I could hear the voices of the Japanese and the occasional shot. I could not fall asleep because I was worried, I may snore and give myself away. I lay there exhausted for those two nights. My heart was racing so fast when I heard the voices, I thought it would erupt out of my chest. The smell of rotting jungle hid the smell of my sweat, urine and the shit that sat in my underwear. I'd moved nothing but my eyeballs for the first terrifying night. My jungle sores stung from moving through the bush. Everything is sharp, every leaf and piece of high grass. It all cuts like a paper cut and then the sweat and the dirt gets in and the skin can't recover in the humidity and you get sores. I had one canteen of water and this was gone by the morning of the third day. I had a compass and one of those maps on a silk handkerchief and so I thought of trying to find the river and head back towards the war. So, my sin brought me to the banks of a river and there up to his waist in the stream was a Japanese soldier washing himself. He had just woken up and had climbed into the water with a bar of soap. His kit and rifle lay on the bank. He spotted me at the same time I saw him so I ran and dived on him in the water. I held him under and drowned him. He struggled like a baby in an unwanted bath. He was small even for a Japanese man. He struggled and fought, but I had good hold of him. Then he died in my hands. Tom got up and walked back to work. I thought about how lucky I had been to be born after the war not to have seen such terrible things. I'm not sure my definition of sin would appease Tom or clear his thoughts or right the wrongs he had done.

Chapter Thirteen

The New Year had drifted in with little celebration. The dark clouds had sat low against the horizon and January made its entrance with promises of a new beginning. Resolutions had been lost in the grimness and relentlessness that every dark January brings. As the month progressed and the new year resolutions, diets and abstentions from alcohol fell by the wayside the days had become slowly brighter. A sense that spring was on the way as snowdrops and crocuses peeped through the soil. February in turn had seen a lift in spirits and a small change in the weather. Now the days could be bright again between the rains and occasional storms. On this February day work for some had been long and physical and now the men sat briefly socialising before returning home to warm fires and central heating. Freddie sat clouded in the mist of moist breath, smoke and speech. Tiredness filled the weary air as the gang sat round the outdoor table under the baren twiggy pergola, perhaps for the last time this winter. Winter brings its own rhythm. It brings the cold and it brings silence. Many people abandon their allotments until early spring, then play catch up with nature in a mad dash to get planting and clearing done. But at the Star Lane things just simply slowed down with the cold. Just like the human metabolism things moved slower. There was less rush. Jobs that would normally take a few hours bulked themselves out to take a few days.

The winter days had been perfect with blue sky and sunshine and now as darkness set in, the sky was feathered by whispers of clouds. The morning frost had melted quickly and the dirt rows of the allotments hung heavy with moisture as day developed with drudgery and hard work. The afternoon welcomed the twilight and then the darkness at just 5.30pm. Two storm lanterns were lit and they hissed away above the four men who sat with large mugs of hot chocolate and what Greggory called an early snifter of dark rum. Smoke from roll-up cigarettes and pipes drifted between the men, still wrapped up to keep in the warmth of physical work. They all wore thick dark overcoats over layers of shirts, jumpers and vests. Each wore either mittens or thick gloves. Freddie, who particularly felt the cold, was wearing two pairs of gloves. Greggory was so wrapped up against the chill in the air, that only the end of his nose protruded out of the hatch of a green balaclava. He had on so many layers that he looked thick set and barrel chested. On this February day work for some had been long and physical and now the men sat briefly socialising before returning home to warm fires and central heating.

"I have got so little done today," said Freddie taking a sip of hot chocolate from his metal mug.

"You managed to look busy all day," replied Hans.

"Oh, I was just pretending to work. There is nothing more difficult than pretending to work. With real work there is an end to it. But there's no end to pretending to work. It goes on forever. I learned that in the RAF."

"No ending to pretending," agreed Tom.

"I watched a documentary last night," started Greggory, "about an upmarket jeweller. Some bloke came into the shop and bought two watches. One for him and one for what looked like his daughter, but was probably his wife. He paid £50,000 for them. He was a property developer, or banker of some sort, like his lordship over there." Greggory gestured towards the empty plot surrounding Griffin's dapper but empty shed.

"That's immoral." said Tom.

"I knew a jeweller once; he was a patient of mine. Worked in the jewellery quarter in Birmingham. He used to bring me earrings for my wife every now and again. He told me that all jewellery is actually only worth 10% of what you pay for it. A hundred quid ring is only worth a tenner. A thousand-pound brooch is worth a hundred quid. The mark up is that high."

"We're all mugs, aren't we?" said Freddie.

"I'm not," said Tom. "If you want to show love, give them a hug. You don't need to buy affection in this world and if you do, that type of love will only last while the money is flowing. We push this idea into our children from an early age that you can buy happiness and you really can't. If you are always spending on the children to alleviate the fact that you spend no time with them because you are too busy working then you are not a good parent. We hugged our kids all the time. My parents did not do that to us. Never told us they loved us, though we knew they did. I never told my dad I loved him, even when he lay in the hospital dying. I promised myself I'd not be like that with my children."

"Are we planning a jewellery raid next Tom?" asked Hans.

"Certainly not." Tom's reply came quickly and testily.

"Can I join you gentleman?" Everyone turned to see Peter coming in under the pergola. He was heavily wrapped up under trench coat, Villa scarf and thick corduroy trousers. He had a claret coloured bobble hat on his head and a few days stubble on his chin, which he scratched as he came beneath the pergola.

"Of course, Peter, step in. Would you like a hot chocolate?"

"Yes, that would be very nice." Peter sat down in the wicker chair that used to be where George had sat at the head of the table. He had put out his hand to find the back of the chair which had sat in the same place for many years. Peter moved around the allotment from memory. He had a cane but he rarely used it once he was on the main car park he knew where the gate was and where all the trip hazards where.

"A drop of rum?" said Greggory.

"That would be welcome too. Thank you. It has been a beautiful day. A rare winter's treat. How is the work going?"

"We were just discussing Freddie's lack of progress today and his failure with the Protestant work ethic," said Hans.

"Work is good for the soul isn't that right Peter? You are the allotment philosopher," said Greggory.

"I mainly taught ethics. Back when I could see and I was young," said Peter with a shrug of the shoulders.

"So, tell me Peter," said Tom, rising to the opportunity to get a discussion going on what was currently troubling his mind, "What makes a good man?"

Freddie looked at Greggory. It was a look of some disquiet for Tom had been mumbling for weeks that the Allotment Gang was the past and it was all a big mistake. Tom had been melancholic for a while and they were not sure whether it was the death of his wife that was causing this or the loneliness. Although he seemed to be having a good time with Marianne from the library and when he did talk, it was usually about her.

"Life is about being happy and the rest is just muddling through isn't it surely?" said Freddie. "When were you happiest, Greggory?"

"I am always happy. I work on being happy. Happiness is like friendship. You work at it. Sometimes people get right up my nose and I accept that because they are my friends and we take the rough with the smooth. But I was most happy in my life in a place at the time we called Port A."

"Where was that?" said Hans

"I can tell you now Hans but I'd have been shot in 1943 for telling you. Loch Ewe up in the Scottish Highlands. We would sail up there from Liverpool with our cargo of Sherman tanks for the Russians and wait in the loch for the other ships to arrive and make up a convoy. We were given shore leave normally before the start of the convoy. Most of us were scared stiff and needed a drink or two to fortify us against what was coming. I was on one of those American Liberty ships that they built in a matter of days. I had been on one before and ran aground in South Africa. I think the wreck is still there. They were really basic inside and my duty was to service the radios on them all while we waited for the convoy to form. I spent a lot of time looking out across the island safe behind the U- boat nets and under the big anti-aircraft guns. They had a Nissan hut attached to a house that they called the village hall. We went dancing with the local girls. The RN commander made it clear that the locals were all god fearing Scottish free church types and would stand for no messing from grubby matelots. We were to be on our best behaviour ashore and if we behaved badly, we would be sat in our liberty ship until the convoy sailed. I met a young woman called Roisin. Long curly red hair and a beautiful face matted with freckles. Just lovely. She danced with me all night. Nothing happened afterwards, no hanky-panky, just a wonderful night carefree in the arms of a beautiful woman. I think I believed I was going to die up in the arctic alone and without having lived enough life. But I survived to tell the tale today. What about you Freddie?"

"I like my motorbikes as you know, and I guess I was most happy, apart from now in your sweet company."

Freddie leant over and gave Greggory a one-armed hug.

"I guess it was the early 60s and I had gone over to the Isle of Mann on the old steam packet out of Liverpool. I rode the big

Triumph on Mad Sunday. That was before the fear of dying set in. I drove that beast like a demon. Two fellas died the same day. Someone always dies on Mad Sunday. We used to go to the Ace café in London and sit around looking tough with the biker vicar, Sherwood he was called. He was the boss of the 59 Club and had a BSA. We were church going bikers, a real mix. The local roughians liked me because I'd been a pilot in the war and drove my bike well. I did not get any grief from the younger ones. You could eat your fill in that café for two shillings. Pie and chips for 1 and 8 and the teaspoons were chained to the table the same as Marco's. It was a good time helping out, trying to keep the younger lads from getting into trouble and killing themselves. A far cry from our local church. I was just trying to do my bit in a positive way, you know, to make the world a better place and enjoy myself with the bikes. All the girls were very pretty which helped, I remember that well."

"Being a good man is not all about happiness," said Peter. "Although happiness is a product of being a good man and a good man is the basis for being a good citizen so says Socrates and Plato."

"Eudaimonia?" said Hans.

"Indeed, happiness and wellbeing are the highest aim of moral conduct and thought. We have a set of important virtues by which to lead your life and these must be in balance."

"How does robbing banks fit into this?" said Tom.

A hush fell on the group. Peter could feel the looks passing from man to man. He had heard enough over the past year to know that these old men had been involved in some very unusual activities. The late comings and goings, the vehicles that were locked up in the garage, never to be heard again, the smell of gunmetal oil.

"Give it a rest Tom," said Freddie with a sigh.

Hans under his breath whispered: "Theft is a mean, and robbery a shameless thing; and none of the sons of Zeus delight in fraud and violence, or ever practiced, either."

"Go on Peter. What are the virtues that I should be aiming to balance?" said Freddie.

"Plato, as Hans has just quoted, believed that the virtues needed to be constantly worked upon to make the true good man. Let's see if I can remember them. Courage, temperance, liberality, munificence, good temper, wittiness, modesty, sincerity, just resentment, civility. I can't remember them all. Needless to say, stick with those and everyone will think you are a top bloke."

"How is your sister Peter? We have not seen her for a while?" said Hans.

"Oh, she is still looking for a good man, but I suspect Plato's virtues come second place to being able to tango and buy her nice things. She will be picking me up later. Anyway fellas, I need to trim all the lavender hedges. It's a job that I have been needing to do for weeks. Thank you for the hot chocolate." Peter stood up and walked out of the light of the hurricane lamps and into what now seemed complete darkness though Peter registered no change.

"Do you think he knows?" said Greggory after Pete had gone and a snipping sound could be heard across the allotment.

"He should do, if Tom keeps blathering his mouth," said Freddie.

Tom stood up and announced that he had a date with a gravestone and left. The others discussed Tom's wellbeing for another thirty minutes before leaving Peter alone cutting hedges under the stars.

Peter's diary

I hit a wall today. Blindness fever is like gaol fever except that I have audio books, good food, friends, wine and the garden to indulge myself in. My sister told me that in 15 years she will be 72 years old and that made me think that I will be in my 70's then too. What life have I already lived, how much time have I got left.? I feel a little lost by all this. It feels that I'm in a midnight of the soul and itching to do and be rather than just consume and not see. At least my friends are having excitement in their lives or so it seems. I tried to plan my tomorrow because today has been very much the same as all the other days. As Top Cat said "Nothing to do and all day to do it". Tom is in a bad state and he keeps coming to me for advice. I've replaced James as a spiritual advisor which is difficult when my only knowledge of Christianity is from the writings of Kierkegaard. I think he needs to sound off on somebody and he knows that James will not give him the answers he needs. I had wracked my brains after the story of the killing of the Japanese soldier to find some form of philosophical solace for him. I used Augustine and how he believed that the City of Men was a brutal, unjust place where no one could achieve moral perfection since that was the prerequisite of the divine. Instead, Tom should think about the kingdom of God instead and this would be a place where he could be forgiven of his sins and good would finally dominate and virtue would reign. He seemed content with that knowledge. He smiled at me and said did I know you can't hum and hold your nose at the same time? Then clapped me on the back and went off to his sprouts. I can't work him out at all.

Chapter Fourteen

Winter gave way to Spring and Tom sat and watched the blackbirds picking the worms from the beds. One particular bird visited Tom's allotment each day scratching at the soil and even getting in the pots and disturbing the Saxifrage, the blue bells, the snowdrops and even the potato plants; his first earlies he always grew in bags. But this particular bird would cast a beady eye on Tom rolling a cigarette and bounce along the path and hop into a potato bag and then from one bag to the next emerging with a beak of worms. She was a particularly industrious mother and seemed to be taking worms and other insects to two nests at the same time. Tom wondered if she was just a charitable soul or had made two nests and confused herself when interlopers had usurped one of them. The birds always gave Tom pleasure. His allotment was strung with feeders of all sorts. The slit feeders filled with Niger seeds just for the goldfinches. The standard seeds for the blue tits, already spring plump and the sparrows and Green Finches. They would peck out a few seeds onto the ground below them, before they found the seed they wanted. Two fat pigeons, too large for the feeders waited expectantly beneath the finches and tits who discarded as many seeds as they consumed. They were picking at the feeders like disappointed children over a meal too heavy with healthy options. At one-point Tom thought the small birds were sharing the seeds with the pigeons. Large homemade fat balls fed the Starlings and all the birds were weary of the shadow of the Sparrow Hawk which regularly visited the fields and woods around the allotments. Two slim wooden tubes with grated metal sheets held the nuts which the birds had to work hard for. Beyond the trees there was a gravel pit which was used by fishermen. Here stood an elegant heron who would let you get within a few meters of it before it unfurled its wing and raised its neck towards the sky only to settle again on the other side of the pit. The heron could be occasionally found on the allotment moving leggily between the crops looking for frogs and toads.

The fields had started to become meadows of green and yellow filled with buttercups and dandelions. The sound of the mechanised plough could be regularly heard turning great swathes of soil and preparing the land for the bounty of the summer. The first bees buzzed lazily and had to be rescued from early exhaustion with spoons and plates filled with sugary water placed out by a tender heart that knew the value of the bee to the English countryside. Down the lane to the Star Inn the verges were filled with Daffodils now starting to turn as the spring fully set in. Their yellow heads bobbing in the air and turning each day to follow the sun. There is nothing as sunny and welcoming, Tom thought, than a daffodil after the winter's cold and dark. Brambles began to dress the hedges with thorny growth and the trees unfurled their new leaves as diaphanous as any green could be and as fresh as the top of a new born child's head. The air slowly filled with tree pollen and the chesty colds of the winter were replaced by the wheezing coughs of early onset hay fever. The browns had turned to greens when the sun emerged and lit up the world with welcome beauty, colour and warmth. At the allotments heavy coats were removed and placed on door pegs while thick woollen shirts remained for the air was still cold, especially in the morning or out of the sunshine. The spring brought not just fresh growth and a sense of a new beginning. A new start as part of the rhythm of the world and the men bent over shovels, spades, hoes and rakes scraped and dug the earth with the same rhythms as one with the nature that surrounded them.

The Allotment Gang had almost forgotten the excitement of the late summer and spring as new work had busied them. Tom walked into the library where Marianne was sitting at the desk reading a story to a small child on her knee. She wore a silky dress in blue, with white embroidered flowers. Whenever someone complimented her on her clothes, she always replied the same way: "Oh this old thing, I got it in a sale."

She was always well dressed and always wore dresses. No one had ever seen her in so much as a pair of slacks. She was one of those women who always looked as if they had just left the hairdressers. Marianne was elegant in her beauty and her tallness allowed her to wear almost anything. She had always been slightly uncomfortable by being tall. If she was in the company of a man, particularly a man she liked and who was the same height or smaller than her, she had this way of crossing one leg behind the other to reduce her height. She didn't think men like tall women. For someone who radiated elegance and charm she could be a little anxious. Marianne was able to make anyone feel that they were the most important and interesting person in the room and this gift of charm was something that endeared her to everyone she met. Tom walked past giving her a smile, Marianne winked back at him. He felt his heart lift. She continued to read the story to the child. Tom was carrying a briefcase with £6000 in it. He had decided to say that this had come from an anonymous benefactor and that Marianne should ask no questions. But he knew he'd never get past her curiosity and so told a story of an old couple who died and left the money to the village community fund.

The library was saved with a donation of £6000 and a deal with the council to sell the building to a group of Trustees for a single penny. The library would continue to open with a stream of volunteers from the community. £6000 would keep the lighting on and books on shelves for at least four years until a grant could be found to make sure it would continue further. The Conservative leader of the council, himself a businessman, thought this was a good news story and showed that the public could maintain a service that the council should be running at no real cost to the taxpayer. So, one late winter Friday morning the leader of the council Grant Thompson rolled up with the Member of Parliament and a photographer from the local paper to get his actions suitably rewarded with acclaim from the local papers. "Tomo saves the day" said the oily headline in the Advertiser. All this had been achieved but now Tom had the job of explaining the £6000 in cash to Marianne.

*

Freddie had been out of sorts for a few weeks until one of the gang asked him what was the matter and was shown a letter from the Chairman of the Alms Houses Trust. Freddie lived in one of its houses. The trust had eight Victorian stone cottages, all in a single terrace. They had been built for farm labourers by the Thistleton family, the local landowners. When old man Cyril Thistleton had died in 1950, he gave the cottages to a trust. The trust had maintained the buildings and had added bathrooms and indoor plumbing. Freddie had a middle cottage with a small white wooden porch. The conversions in the 1960s had made the two up two down cottages into single bedroom properties. They were pleasant enough homes, dry and bright, but were very small. The letter talked about financial problems with the trust and debts that had accrued and been mismanaged over many years. Freddie, like the other tenants, had not been aware of any problems. The upshot was that the houses were going to be sold on the open market to pay off the debt. A property developer could buy the buildings and start to charge market rents instead of the rents that the current tenants enjoyed. The trustees had consulted lawyers but there was nothing they could do to save the sale of the property. Freddie could not afford the higher rent and would soon be without a home.

A week after the letter had arrived the properties were placed on the open market at £200,000 working out at £25,000 for each. Though the houses could not be bought individually; the original mandate stating the properties must remain intact at sale.

"Or," said Greggory, "the trust receives a £200,000 investment leaving it to manage the houses as Alms houses."

He smiled at Freddie. Freddie could see the glint of mischief in Greggory's eye. "We would have to do a bank to get that sort of cash and you can't just give £200,000 in cash to any organisation without it drawing up suspicion," he said crossly.

"It's called money laundering," Hans said later that night as the Allotment Gang reconvened over a bottle of Jameson's whiskey.

"How does that work?" said Tom.

"Well, you take the cash and you have to put it into numerous accounts and then pay off the Trustees from those accounts. But the banks will be instantly suspicious of that amount of cash being put into the bank. Especially if it's been stolen from the bank in the first place."

"You are not considering doing a bank, are you Freddie?" said Tom, raising his eyebrow at the thought and complexity of robbing a bank."

"Nowhere else carries that sort of money. We would be robbing petrol stations and post officers for months and would get caught when our luck ran out."

"But how would we launder that sort of money?"

"We could create a charity appeal. Ask for donations and launder the cash through those donations. Set up some separate children's accounts at the post office. They do that sort of thing. Build those up over time and transfer the money to pay off a loan. Oh, I don't know there must be some way of doing this."

"Anonymous donations will not hack it, especially of its cash and you can't launder a hundred grand through children's accounts," said Hans.

"We rob the bank, launder the money through a charity and buy the alms houses. Otherwise, some master of the universe type from London is going to come along and buy them up and kick out all the tenants. Cyril will be turning in his grave."

"You make it sound so simple Greggory old boy," said Freddie, "Did you know Cyril?"

"No."

"I did, absolute bastard of a man. Cared not one jot about anyone but himself. When he died his wife, bless her, created the trust in his name. It was a sort of tax evasion, I think. Cyril's memory lives on in this legacy. But he was a vile man."

"When I was a lad a gang of us went onto one of his fields where we took a sledge to run down the hill on. He turned up with his own kids and chased us off the field. 'Get off my land' he shouted. Horrible man. Couldn't even allow a gang of kids to sledge in the snow."

"This time we will need to do a lot of work on the planning."

"Maybe we could change the name of the trust?"

"I think we have more pressing plans than to eliminate that man's name from history," said Hans.

Tom moved the conversation back to the job in question: "The big bank in the centre of Bromsgrove has two entrances. The back one on that little car park and the front one onto the High Street. All the mortgages and loans are organised through there and there would probably be a lot of cash because it sits among all those shops."

"Bromsgrove it is then," said Freddie.

"We have to take more care this time," said Hans, "I was reading in a medical journal that they can now test for DNA and the police are introducing this as a way to prosecute criminals. The slightest piece of your sweat or hair, maybe even droplets in breath, can be picked up from surfaces. They can check these against your own DNA, it's a simple swab test. If there is a match then you would have to explain how this was part of a crime scene. It is better than any finger print. So, this time it is surgical gloves and hair nets and we will destroy the clothing. We have to be a bit more professional."

"The greatest protection we have is not making mistakes and our ordinariness. The last people they will come looking for will be us," said Freddie.

"As long as we don't make any mistakes," agreed Greggory.

The discussions ended abruptly as Freddie announced that he had just seen the first house martin fly over the hedge, dip low over the vegetable patch and enter one of the many mud nests under the eaves of the Star Inn Pub. The return of the house martins was eagerly awaited each year because they provided the evening entertainment through the summer months for the old men. Freddie would often say that if he could have flown half as well in the war he would never have been shot down.

Each evening above the growing plants the house martins put on the most dramatic display of aerial acrobatics. Sweeping, diving, banking sharply and occasionally swooping down into the full water troughs and drinking on the wing. The birds were much celebrated and the cheeping noise that they made seemed to enhance the experience even more. Even Peter would pause and listen.

"I swear the bugger did a barrel roll before entering the nest," said Hans.

"It has flown a long way to come back here, the poor thing must be worn out," replied Tom.

"I am glad they are back. It's a bit later than usual but they are here now," said Freddie.

*

You want me to help you build what? Rosie was not one to be shocked by anything, but she seemed truly aghast at what Greggory had just asked.

"You have some explaining to do, Greggory. Are you embarking on a freedom fighting plot?" They stood between the sheds. Greggory had two mugs of tea in his hand and had called Rosie over to join him minutes before. Tom and Hans had already hatched a plan for the bank but there was a technical problem and when there was a technical problem, then Rosie was the person to deal with it. Tom thought Rosie would be game. Let's face it she was game for most things and it's not like she will be putting herself in danger. She is not coming on the job. He had said. They had discussed it all the night before and this morning it was left to Greggory to recruit another member of the Allotment Gang. He was unsure how Rosie would react, but he knew that she had adventure in her soul and that after some initial consternation she would indeed join the gang.

"Sit down Rosie. This is going to take some explaining. Rosie sat on the bench below the pergola. The table was littered with mugs and newspapers. A breeze blew between the gap in the sheds. The afternoon had taken on a chill and at least the predicted rain had held off.

"There is no easy way of explaining this". Greggory said, "We have been robbing from the rich to sort of give to the poor."

"Who exactly is we?" Rosie said waspishly, it was the only question Rosie could think of.

"Tom, me, Hans and Freddie." Said Greggory now starting to look a little sheepish.

"Freddie?" said Rosie.

"All of us, we sort of got a bit wrapped up in the excitement of it all."

"The excitement of what Greggory?" Rosie had suddenly taken on the tone of a distraught parent or a schoolteacher. Neither of which she was pleased by.

"We have been doing a few robberies and giving the money away to the poor." Rosie looked on then a smile began to trace across her mouth.

"Oh, Greggory!" Rosie began to laugh, but when she could see that Gregory was being absolutely serious, she stopped.

"You are not kidding, are you?" Greggory shook his head from side to side.

"It's been sort of exhilarating to be doing something exciting and worthy at last." he said.

"Stealing isn't a worthy pastime."

"But it sort of is when you are doing it for other people."

"Who has benefitted?" asked Rosie.

"Well, the church has a new electrical system." Rosie's eyes rolled upwards; Greggory continued. "We have saved the library. And a few people have had some cash donations to see them through difficult times."

What have you done to get the money?

We robbed a post office and a petrol station. Now we need your help. Well to be honest you have already helped.

"How have I already helped?

"You made one of the getaway cars run faster."

"So, you lied to me and made me complicit in a robbery."

"Sorry" said Gregory.

"Sorry" whispered Rosie. "How do you need my further help?"

"We need to burn a van out so that there is no evidence, but the van must burn after we have left it. If it burns while we are there someone might see us or take details of the second car. I can make a firebomb, but I don't know how to detonate it on a timer. You once told me that you kept a box of things from the war. You said you had an old SOE pencil detonator. Would it still work? Could we have it.? The money is going to save the alms-houses. Save Freddie's home. It's a just cause."

"So let me get this right, you have misled me into being an accomplice in a robbery now you want to make me into a bomb maker."

"You will not get caught. No one will know you are involved. It's almost risk free."

Rosie gave Gregory one of her mischievous looks. He knew this so well.

Two hours later Rosie was in her shed with Gregory on the potting table was a can of petrol, some rags, a vial of acid and two World War Two SOE pencil timers.

Peter's diary

How important is sleep. My diary always talks about sleep. I no longer have the deep blackness of sleep, dream free, deep relaxation, fragile. Now it is filled with stories and adventures, not always nice. But I can see in my dreams. I can see faces and flowers and landscapes. Sometimes when I sit in the allotment at night, I can see all that is around me. Even though the darkness makes even the sighted struggle. It is darkest beneath the trees and I feel the wicker of my chair mottle the skin on my back for I sit there too long.

The others are conspiring again. I know what they are going to do and I am afraid that they will get hurt or disappear to prison. They believe that they are doing a good deed but carrying guns again after all these years of peace in their lives is not good for the soul. They are an accident waiting to happen but I cannot interject and criticise because I am not really a party to the gang. So, I sit instead in darkness living for sensuality and the pleasures that drink, food, touch, smell, taste and exercise bring. My arms ache from the digging and carrying. My shoulders feel worn and I wonder what I look like now bent from toil sat here in the darkness. Just a series of momentary pleasures making me feel alive and that life is still worth it. Nothing has changed for mankind in all the centuries. We still want the same pleasures. Exactly the same pleasures: sex, food, entertainment, stories, drink, laughter, conversation. Nothing has ever really changed. Later I thought about my brother and how he died a pointless death. Coming through the war only to be buried alive digging for antiquities in a Cheshire midden. I miss him very much. I miss his laughter and I miss the way he used to wind me up as a boy over dinner until mother would tell him to leave me alone. Just my sister left now. Anyway, the house martins are back all is well with the world.

Chapter Fifteen

Early summer arrived with the promise of something fresh and new, apple trees, all pinks, white and green bobbing effortlessly in the softest of breezes. Their branches conducted the slowest of symphonies in the warm air. Already pollen danced and caught in the early morning sunlight, while precocious, busy insects fought for air space in an already busy flight pattern. Just the drowsy hum of bees could be heard for the moment. The strawberries in their neat rows would be painted brightly soon and the souls of the allotment looked forward to ripe cherries to fill the evening's relaxation. No morning mists covered the landscape, late bluebells nodded in the woods and a nightingale could be heard singing deep among the trees. The nearby dew-soaked meadows were filled with buttercups and daisies, struggling to make themselves noticed between the grasses. They shone towards the sunshine. Lambs slowly fattened in the fields, while their mothers curled against the base of hedges, chewing endlessly. Millie the cat left a trail of darkened grass, as her belly stripped the grass of the dew, as she prowled for field mice. She paused thinking twice about lying down in the wet field, choosing instead to jump the fence and head for the comfort and shade of the Pergola inside the allotments.

Wednesday was considered the day off at the allotment. So, it was not unusual for little work to be done. Rarely did anyone tend to their plants. The Star Lane allotments became a place of quiet, stillness and peace. Only the birds danced around in the air and hopped eagerly about on the ground. The plants, unencumbered by fussing hands, were left to grow undisturbed. The green beans grew longer, the tomatoes changed from yellow to green, the bees pollinated busily and the herbs infused the air with scents. No work Wednesday was not really a rule, it was just a convenient warning, that if you wanted company then you would be disappointed. No one would be there. Hans was with the Archery Club, Freddie would be fishing, Tom would be doing his weekly shop and calling in at the library to see Marianne. Gregory would be visiting his friend Lynn, even Griffin's gardener had the day off. Only Rosie came to work on a Wednesday, not because she wanted to be alone, but more because she didn't like either rules, warnings or even notions. It had always been so. If there was a rule, she thought was pointless, then she would actively go out to break it. Rosie did not play by other people's rules or notions about behaviour. She never had and never would. Rosie did what she wanted. If she wanted a pint she would go for a pint, if she wanted fish and chips she would go to the chippy, if she wanted new clothes or even a new motorbike, she would just go and sort it out.

On Wednesday, the big Triumph was to be found in the Allotment car park and would sit ticking as it cooled. More often than not Rosie would be sitting in a deckchair sipping hot Bovril on her plot. On summer days she would sit in shorts and a t- shirt, reading one of her favourite books in either French or German. Then do the puzzles in *Le Monde* or *Le Figaro*, which Stanley at the paper shop would get in specially for her. They may have been two days late, but he always managed to secure one. Occasionally, he would get a *Bild*, but that was more difficult to source and was expensive. Rosie would pick the paper up on Wednesday morning and hope for good reading weather. There is, she thought, something very comforting about sitting in a striped deck chair. Something quintessentially English. She toyed with the idea of knotting her red handkerchief and wearing it on her head, like the men in the saucy cartoon postcards sold at the seaside. Rosie was self-contained and free of the trappings and restrictions of other people's opinions. Growing old disgracefully was her motto. She contentedly sat reading her paper as the house martins flew around her, cheeping excitedly at the number of insects available to them for dinner. Rosie found nothing suspicious in the emptiness of the allotments. However, Hans was not at archery club, he would say he was fishing with Freddie and then later joining Tom for a pint, Tom would appear at the library later than normal telling Marianne that he had gone for a drink in the Sugarbrook pub, after the food shop that he had actually done the day before. Greggory would turn up to Lynn's house late too, saying he had been working on a car for a friend. They were all alibis of a sort.

Five miles away the Bank in Bromsgrove was open for market day business. It had two entrances. A front entrance on the High Street and a rear entrance from a small car park. The floor of the Bank was a large open space divided with a row of teller's desks set behind a thick glass screen which was 8 foot high. Below the glass were panels of oak. Behind the screen, there was an open plan office space with desks with leather chairs and at the back behind a screen, onto which were pinned notices, sat the vault. The top of a big green steel door could be seen over the screen. Eight men and women sat on desks or at the tellers' hatches. No one spoke. It was a place of quiet and work. There were no frivolous conversations between them, it was as if all the fun of life had been drained out of the room. This is how Mr Barnes liked his bank to be run. Barnes was an ex-grammar school boy from the local council estate who had done well for himself. He won a scholarship and went to Birmingham University, there he studied accountancy and excelled at having few friends and reading French literature while everyone else went to parties. He had joined the bank in the late 60s and had become the manager not long after. He was quiet, almost monosyllabic in conversation and he saw language as a means to order people to do his wishes. When the Allotment Gang entered the bank, he was in his office berating a junior clerk, whose cash till had been three pence out at the end of the previous day. He enjoyed admonishing his staff, particularly the young men who he saw as feckless and vain dandies in their shiny modern cut suits.

On the public side of the bank there was a nice thick green carpet and the walls were covered in oak panels onto which were neatly stuck advertisements for mortgages and loans. The screen, dividing the tellers from the customers, stretched upwards but left a space before the ceiling giving the gap between the two sections of the bank an airy, if less secure feel. Only two tills were open, so a small queue had formed in front of each. At the front of one queue was a long-haired young man with big bags of coins which he was delivering from a local pub. He looked nervous because he was driving his boss's car, which was a large Volvo estate, and he had been worried about getting it parked in the small car park. Behind him stood an elderly lady who was sighing loudly. The other queue was made up of a gentleman in a pin striped suit and a boy wearing grey shorts and a school blazer. They were being served by Lisa Foggart who had worked at the bank for ten years and now at the age of thirty was the most trusted and efficient worker on the staff. She was within arm's reach of the only door that linked the two parts of the bank. Lisa was a very intelligent young woman and had initially trained to be a medical secretary, but found the aggressive and often very ill patients trying. She did not want their misfortune to spoil her otherwise happy life. She moved through time with grace and calmness being content with all things. But the final straw for her medical secretarial career was a particularly aggressive and angry woman, who spoke to her in the most demeaning way, as only one older woman can speak to another younger far more attractive woman. Lisa had 'lost it' told her to fuck off and walked out of the surgery office never to return. Within a day she had a new job as a trainee clerk at the bank and over the past ten years through industry and hard work had risen to Chief Teller. Lisa wore her thick dark hair in a bun and only released it when she slept at night. She had a strong face with dark eyes and full lips accentuated by her hair pulled tight across her head. She always dressed well and wore very tight skirts and shirts which emphasised her body. The eyes of the younger men in the bank could be seen following her around the office whenever she moved. She was as desirable as she was single. Lisa's temperament and her training meant she was the best person that day to meet an armed robber. Her looks alone were disarming. She knew in her heart that no man was the match for her and she would always act in her own best interest. She could be submissive, but this was show, because she would put up a good fight if needed. No man would be the better of her. She had her life planned out; she would inherit her father's farm. She would have the dogs and the horses and the occasional man in her life and only when needed.

Into this place of calm and work burst Freddie, Tom and Hans. They wore identical blue boiler suits, face masks, surgical gloves and heavy work boots. Tom brandishing a pistol went straight to the central table and stepping up from the chair, took a commanding position over the room. Freddie and Hans shouting "Get down on the floor, get down on the fucking floor," charged through the queues. Freddie stopped to help the old lady to her knees as only a gentleman would. She was the last to lie down. By then Tom was in front of Lisa Foggart with a shotgun pointed directly through the glass screen at her chest.

"You are not going to shoot me, are you Mister?" said the boy in the blazer now flat on his face with his hands across the back of his head.

"No just lie down on the floor lad and we will be out of here in a few seconds," replied Hans, sounding more American than he ever had. He had been practising losing his German accent by watching American soaps and cowboy films.

"Don't take my money Mister. I am saving for a Raleigh racing bike." The boy implored earnestly.

"Just lie down lad and you can keep your money." Hans said, in a most reassuring tone for an armed robber now with a hint of John Wayne in his voice.

"It's just like the movies," the little boy said to himself breathlessly.

Tom shouted at the teller to open the door. Lisa Foggart did exactly what she had been taught to do. She slid neatly from her seat leaning to the right and proceeded to open the door between the two halves of the bank while using her left hand to press the panic button which was hidden under the counter. The door flashed open and Hans armed with the sawn-off shotgun and Freddie with the service revolver burst into the office space. Tom remained on the table in front keeping an eye on the customers now all visibly cowering on the floor.

"Everyone on the floor, face down and no one gets hurt." shouted Freddie to the clerks.

He swung the shotgun around the room and watched each of the banking staff get onto the floor. They knew they had less than a minute. Hans ran past and went straight to the vault.

Lisa Foggart defiantly sat down on her chair. No man was going to tell her to lie down. Freddie wandered his eyes up her shapely stockinged legs and decided she could stay where she was. The distraction was enough for one of the tellers to set his alarm off as well.

The safe door was open. It had been left open by the same young man who had lost three pence in his till from the day before. He was always leaving it open. In fact, the vault door was left open most of the time during the working day. It was one of the things Greggory had noticed when he did the recce of the bank over several alternative days in the weeks before the raid. Inside the vault room in bundles of notes was the reason for all the madness and risk. Hans smiled from behind the surgical mask, false beard, blonde wig and dark glasses. He started packing the canvass sailors' shoulder bags. In went the cash, thousands of pounds. Scooped up by his gloved hand from the shelf and straight into the sack. He only took the ten and twenty-pound notes. He left all the green pound notes and the blue five-pound notes. He noticed that his queen looked up at him from the face of the notes disapprovingly.

"Twenty seconds." shouted Freddie.

One sack was filled and Hans started on the second. The adrenalin pumping round his body. He could feel his hands shake. He thought he had never felt so alive. Not since the moment in the Falaise Pocket just before he had surrendered in 1944.

"Ten seconds!" shouted Freddie.

Don't be greedy Hans thought as he got the second bag three quarters filled. On the call of 'NOW' from Freddie. He stopped. Leaving two shelves stacked with money remaining in the vault he ran back into the office throwing the second sack at Freddie who caught it with his free hand which immediately dropped with the weight of the money. They turned and ran out of the office and into the public space where Tom stood. No one had come into the bank. It had taken four minutes from entry to leaving. Just like they had planned. The police sirens could be heard approaching from a distance, probably a mile away still. Out into the car park they dove into a waiting Ford transit van, a flurry of adrenalin and action and off they went, Greggory drove slowly doubling back, taking ten turns into different roads to take them barely half a mile from the bank. On Manor Crescent, a quiet cul de sac with only three houses on it was the second vehicle, a large grey Mercedes estate taken two nights before. The van pulled up behind it. They waited to check to see if there was anyone about. There was no one.

Tom said calmly: "Let's go."

They clambered out of the van, still in the disguises and into the car. Immediately Greggory switched on the engine by twisting the wires in the open ignition and the gang drove off. The men stripped down to their underpants and stuffed all the clothes and disguises into black bin bags which were waiting on the seats for them. The last thing into the bag were the hair nets and wigs. They kept the surgical gloves on. The three guns were unloaded and put into a black sports bag with West Bromwich Albion in white letters written on the side.

No one spoke. But they sweated and panted as they got into green work overalls, corduroy trousers, check shirts and shoes and boots. They quickly remerged from the chrysalis of crime into the respectability of four elderly men. Greggory drove along the country lanes and back into the town they had left only a few minutes before. Two police cars raced past them in the opposite direction.

"Just a group of old men off to the pub," Joked Freddie, but the tension in the vehicle was so acute that not even nervous laughter was appropriate.

A mile away the car pulled into a row of garages on the Charford estate. Greggory drove straight into the garage and then got out and closed the garage door behind them.

Just at this point, the van that had been abandoned exploded into smoke and flames. A homemade acid detonator clock had ignited two small tanks of petrol filled with rags. The van first smoked vigorously and then burned quickly. By the time the fire engine arrived there was little left of the van. A burnt-out shell sat on melted tyres. By the time Savage and Hunter got to the van, it was blackened and warm.

The men left the garage one at a time using the door at the back and walked down the passageway and onto the road to the Sugarbrook pub. Only Greggory stayed. A large barrel of acid sat in one corner of the garage and into it went the gloves, face masks, socks, hair nets and wigs. Greggory used a pair of tailor's scissors to cut down the clothes into blue strips and put them into an old potato sack to burn later. When he was satisfied that all the disguises were in the barrel, he swept the floor and hoovered the inside of the car. He wiped all the surfaces of the interior of the car with strong disinfectant. He replaced the number plates with the real ones and removed the two thick black stripes which ran down the sides of the car. He cleaned off the sticky adhesive that remained. The large Mercedes estate car would be returned to a garage in the next village before the owners returned from their holiday. After two hours of work, he picked up the money, now in leather saddle bags and attached them to the back of his moped. He made sure the air venting pump was working and discharging the smell of the acid out of a long chimney on the roof. He stopped outside and sniffed the air; he could smell nothing.

In the pub down the road the three men stood in the saloon bar, the adrenalin still rushing round their bodies. Freddie's hand shook slightly as he held his pint of Marstons Pedigree. They took their beers to a corner table next to the Space Invader machine, which tunelessly made the noise 'zid, zid, zid, zid', as they drank. Hans opened a packet of dry roasted nuts and they sat quietly looking at each other. Freddie smiled and they all smiled back.

"Well, that was the most extraordinary thing I have done since the war," said Tom.

"In all the years I have known you two I have never once heard you swear." said Hans

"Oh, I just thought it would add somewhat to the general ambiance of the occasion." smirked Freddie, winking his eye at Hans.

"Plus, Tom is the only socialist I have ever met who doesn't like people," said Freddie.

From across the saloon lounge the young bartender watched as the three old men roared with laughter. 'Silly old buggers,' he thought.

Peter's diary

I had an interesting conversation today with Tom. I had been picking runner beans and I was enjoying the sunshine on my face. I think lifting my face to feel the warmth of the sun is one of the great pleasures in life. I can look directly at the sun and I can see it admittedly only as white light in a grey haze. But I can see it. The sense of sight has not been totally lost to me and the memories of what things look like remain with me. My runner beans are delicious especially if I cut them thinly, but I must watch that I don't cut my finger. Rosie kindly bought me a sort of chain mail glove that I use in the kitchen that protects me from slicing myself open. Tom stood over me and shaded out the sunshine. From his voice I could tell that he had a look of concern on his face. I never knew Tom when I could see so I imagined his face a little like a reader of a book does. Tom said he needed to chat to me as a philosopher and that he could not speak with the vicar because the issue was of a sensitive nature and he trusted my judgement not to gossip about what he would ask. Afterwards I could see why he was so conflicted and could not talk to the vicar. This was an issue of morality and ethics he said and that his church and his God would already have a view on his behaviour. Quite quickly I realized why. So, Tom and some friends and I think I can work out who they may have been behind a series of robberies which he justified as a means to provide the poor with alms. He used the word alms. He said no one had been physically hurt in these robberies though I pointed out that the psychological impact on his victims could be really bad. He agreed with this but wanted to follow up on previous conversations about what makes a good man. Was he a Benthamite? He asked was his action for the greater good of the society he lived in. It was all very strange. I taught philosophy for many years and never had a confessional before. He said that the early philosophers were really like our modern-day plethora of self-help guides and gurus. The question of course is how should one live? was what he wanted to hear. I ran through Aristotle and Plato and a sort of crash course in ethics. But in the end, I could only tell him that what he had done was wrong and he should really stop or he would be both judged in a court of law in the same way that he claimed his church and religion would judge him.

I am no psychologist nor am I able to give him advice. He seemed quite broken by what he had been doing. He asked should he give himself up but then insisted that I don't talk to anyone about this until he had made up his mind. I have to say it's not every day that an elderly gangster comes to seek my advice. I felt more flattered than disturbed. It would explain the late nights comings and goings at the allotment. The others seem content with what they are doing. I side with them; the thrill of life and adventure is what living is all about. I'm not talking of pure hedonism but just doing what is right even when it may be judged as being wrong by society. I'm not even sure society would judge them as wrong. For many they would be heroes. I'm not sure Rosie has wised up to what is going on yet.

I want to be part of it. I want excitement back in my life. But what use is there for a blind bank robber? Or another philosopher in prison.

Chapter Sixteen

The roar of the big Triumph Bonneville engine could be heard loudly even inside the crash helmet, as Rosie sped through the country lanes like a demon. She wore black helmet and black leather trousers and boots. Over the leather jacket was a denim coat with the arms cut off at the shoulders. On the back of the worn denim was stitched the words 'Born to Ride'. Her face was a vision of intense concentration. Rosie used the muscle memory of riding the route to first break and then move through the gears. The changes came naturally and without thought. She relaxed the throttle as she entered the sharper bends then pulled the nose of the bike up as she flew out of the other side. The engine throbbed through her with such power that she felt like she was being lifted off her seat by the acceleration. She knew these roads well and the journey to get the Sunday papers always felt like she was at her beloved TT course on the Isle of Mann. She remained focussed as she took the long slow right-hand bend and charged up the hill, trees flashing by in the corner of her eyes. At the top of the hill, she braked hard before the T junction stopping to let an Austin Princess drive by. Her heavily booted foot touched the road just for long enough to allow the car to pass before she pulled out of the junction. The next three bends she loved to ride through, as she tried to get her padded knee as close to the road surface as she dared. She hit 80mph on the long straight road into Stoke Prior and then slowed down to pass the rows of houses and the police house. Sgt Brian had heard the engine even over the noise of his lawn mower and looked up to recognise Rosie as she passed his home at a legal and sensible 30 mph. "Mad bugger!" he said to himself. At the end of the road, she turned the slow left and did a small jump over the canal bridge at Tardebigge. She felt her stomach lift into her throat as she crossed the hump of the bridge. Now Rosie bit into her bottom lip and lifted the speed again. She felt alive. She felt uplifted. She felt as different from the rest of the people she knew as she could possibly be. As she got closer to the allotments, she could see Freddie ahead of her on his Velocette motorbike. He was on his way to church and was dressed in a dark suit and sat astride the motorbike. Rosie had him in her sights as she drew up closer to him hitting 70mph on the long straight. As she reached him, she gunned the big engine and sped past causing Freddie to wobble. "Fighter pilot my arse," she said through gritted teeth as she pulled away into the distance. Freddie grinned inside his helmet. Everyone loved Rosie. It was just a thing. A mile further down the country lane she pulled left into the small Star Inn car park. She hoped that the Sunday papers would not be smeared with sweat and creases when she unzipped two of them from the front of her jacket. Three more were rolled up, like arrows in a quiver, inside the leather tube across her back. For this was the normal Sunday ritual at the allotments, some went to church, some lay in bed and some went for the newspapers. By the time the others arrived for work the papers would be sat waiting for them on the big oak table made from railway sleepers under the pergola.

Sunday was the best day of the week for Greggory. He was always at the allotments first and then at about ten Rosie would arrive with the papers and he would have a mug of sugary black coffee waiting for her. They would sit and chat for a while and then start on the day's tasks. The others, Tom and Hans would drift in later after church, Hans on his bicycle and Tom often on foot and then Freddie would turn up last, normally on his

Velocette with a novel tucked into the large pocket of his leather coat. They were all a little later than normal because they had had a few drinks on Saturday night to celebrate the news that there was no news. The adrenalin of the previous Wednesday and the inevitable anxieties had meant they had struggled to find sleep until the early hours. Greggory had brought the getaway car and parked it in the single garage next to the allotments. It had already been cleaned and the distinctive black lines had been removed. It no longer looked much like the car from robbery but for colour and make. The distinguishing marks were all lost in Greggory's thorough clean up.

*

Hunter was at work too. He was sitting at ten o'clock that morning at his desk with the newspapers underneath a spiral bound notebook. He was listing the similarities between the three robberies that had occurred so far on his watch. He was starting to believe they were the same gang. The revolver like a cowboy gun had been similarly described by the bank clerk Lisa Foggart. Three men in the gang in the bank and one outside in a vehicle. It was the same as the petrol station. The bastards are getting bolder, thought Hunter.

"What did the child say again, Savage?" Hunter looked over at Savage who was sitting back in his chair with his feet on the desk. He was not happy to be brought into work on a Sunday. It was not the same pay as it had been during the miners' strike and he had planned to get some fresh air and then spend lunchtime in the pub. Savage was sulking.

"Which child? " said Savage, knowing full well what Hunter was referring to.

"The lad in the bank job." replied Hunter testily.

"He said the man with the pistol was really big and had spoken to him about keeping hold of his money for a bike." Savage flicked through his note book.

"A really big man," said Hunter. I guess when you're a kid on the floor looking up, any grown up is a big man."

"Especially when he's holding a shooter boss"

"What about the others?"

"The young bloke from the pub said he didn't really see anything." Savage shuffled through his notebook again. He said "I saw the first man come in shouting that we should get on the floor. I did that and I kept looking at the floor. I was scared that if I looked at him, I would be shot."

"Bloody useless" muttered Hunter.

He did say one of them was an American though. Savage snapped the notebook closed.

"What about the pretty girl? What's her name?" said Hunter.

"Miss Foggart. She's a piece of work, legs all the way to her armpits. She said she set off the alarm as she had been trained to do. She opened the connecting door and let them in. She had a good look at the American and the one with the sawn off."

"And she described the pistol as a cowboy gun. We are waiting on the cameras. The bank manager said it was a service revolver."

"Bingo," said Hunter.

"In and out in three minutes. Only 40 seconds in the vault. Just went for the big notes."

"Were they marked?"

"Yes boss." said Savage.

Hunter picked up the local evening newspaper from the previous day. The headline screamed £200,000 stolen in an armed raid. The reporter had got to the bank just after the police had arrived. A police dispatch radio operator had tipped them off immediately after the 999 calls had come in. He received £50 every time he alerted the editor of the newspaper about a juicy tip off. The story continued breathlessly under the headline and photo of the brave and attractive Miss Foggart. The biggest bank robbery in the history of crime in Worcestershire. Police have no clues who the gang were though a source close to the investigation said that it was probably Birmingham gangsters.

"Shit." said Hunter. "I was in the chief superintendent's office getting a monster while this prick was writing the scoop of his life. Sources close to the investigation my arse."

"We have three more interviews to do tomorrow, Boss. The manager and two others who were in the queue. There's the video to come in too."

"Any news on the vehicle?"

"Only what you could see. Totally burned out. I have some of the forensic bods taking a look at it just in case."

Hunter stared at his list trying to make the connections between the robberies in the hope that something would help them come to a conclusion. It could now be Big Reg, he thought. This was an audacious crime. It was more in his style.

That afternoon Hans drove the getaway car back to the locked garage in the village nearby. Hans wore glasses and a thick fake beard and a bobble hat. The owner was often seen out walking in his bobble hat and to the casual observer Hans was the owner of the car. The garage door key was in the lock as Greggory said it would be. He left the car after a further wipe down and having replaced the ignition, so it did not look tampered with, he strolled away from the house which sat behind thick hedges and walked down the country lane unobserved but for a solitary passing car. He climbed a stile, pulled off the glasses and beard and followed the foot path back to his home four miles away taking his time and swinging his walking stick in a jaunty fashion, knowing the job had been well done. He looked like a sturdy English gentleman out for a pleasant country walk and not, as he imagined, like James Cagney. He thought to himself, with a wry smile, that he was indeed on "top of the world ma". Summer was here and there was proper work to be done. He would be picking potatoes for at least a day. He did not look forward to bending over all day on his knees. He wondered if he could persuade one of the distant grandchildren to come over and help him. He twirled the walking stick in his hand and he marched onwards. I would rather have another visit to the lovely Mrs Simpson, he thought. That could become back breaking work too.

As he arrived at his home there was a young girl standing on his pathway. She was short with dark hair, she had freckles and was overweight. Her Chopper bicycle blocked his garden gate.

"Hello, can I help you young lady?" said Hans.

"Yes, you can. Is that your cat?"

"No, he is called Socks and belongs to the family across the road."

"Can you get it for me?" the girl demanded in a nasty little voice.

"Why?"

"Because I am looking after it and it keeps sitting in the middle of the road and is going to get killed," she said.

"I am sure he will be fine," said Hans

"No, he won't. Will you get him for me?"

"No, he is not your cat."

The young girl crossed her arms in front of her and shrugged her shoulders and pouted her lips.

"You know I have driven my father mad during home schooling?" she replied sullenly.

"Yes, I can see that and I have only just met you." Hans walked wearily to his home. It had been a long few days.

Freddie could see Tom sitting at the table under the pergola between the three sheds at the centre of the allotments. Tom struck a forlorn figure, stooped over a mug of tea and with a sad and faraway look in his eyes. I don't think he has moved all day, thought Freddie. He carried on scraping the brick path with a trowel clearing moss and lichen that had made the pathway slippery underfoot. It was a slow laborious job and one he could do without having to do since his knee was playing him up after the robbery. After an hour Freddie decided to take a break. He boiled the kettle on the gas burner and made himself and Tom a cup of tea. He looked up at the chalked list of jobs to do and muttered to himself "It's never ending." Tom had still not moved from the table until Freddie approached with a fresh mug of tea.

"Chin up fella," said Freddie. Tom looked up and smiled a weary smile.

"Are you feeling ok Tom?" Freddie asked. Tom shrugged his shoulders.

"No," came the reply.

"What is up with you man?" said Freddie, placing the tea in front of Tom. "Here this will cheer you up."

"I feel guilty, Freddie and I feel like I have behaved badly."

"We have all behaved badly, old boy. You just have to muddle through."

"I have justified my," he paused, then said "Our behaviour as a good thing. When stealing and threatening people with guns is anything but a good thing."

"Oh, come on we have had a bit of a wild time, but it is over now. There is no need to do anymore. We achieved what we set out to do and a lot more. There are a few people around here in a much better position than they would have been if we had just carried on growing veg. Come on, we could all do without this guilt trip that you're on. We have had a bit of a lark, our lives have all been more exciting. I've not felt this alive since the war ended. Think of the positives."

"Don't you feel bad?" said Tom. "I can't sleep at all and I just feel that I have done some terrible things and…"

"Can't sleep? I am sleeping like I have been hit over the head by a bag of stars." said Freddie.

"I have lost my direction, Freddie. I know what I have done is deeply wrong and I was thinking of, you know."

"No, I don't know Tom," said Freddie anxiously.

"I think I should give myself up"

"What, to the police? You know we will all go to jail. We will all die in jail." Freddie emphasized the word die. "We are no spring chickens."

"I would not let on who was with me, don't worry."

"Well old chap I am worried." Freddie tried to hide the edge of anger that was welling up in him. "Look, we took the risks because no one in their right mind would come looking for us. We are all old men. Gentlemen even. No criminal record. Pillars of the local community. The only way we would ever have been caught was if we were caught in the act. No policeman would ever work out that a gang of old fellas who spend their weeks growing vegetables could be bank robbers. But if you go and give yourself up, they will start to sniff around you and your friends. There's probably film evidence or even recordings of us. You will open a floodgate, Tom. Imagine what would happen to me with my boyish good looks in a prison." Tom smiled. "Perhaps you are right Freddie. But that was the last one," said Tom.

"Ok," said Freddie. "It is the last one. No more. Now drink your tea, it's going cold and for goodness sake cheer up. Think positively even if you are Britain's public enemy number one." He grinned and patted Tom on the back as he stood from the table and went back to scraping the paths clear. Tom sighed, drank his tea and went to look at the progress of his lettuce crop under the cloches.

That night Greggory lifted the floorboards of his spare room after moving an old rug he had brought back from Peru on one of his many journeys with the merchant navy. The rug showed a Tumi, the sacrificial dagger of the Inca civilization. It was an old and faded rug. One by one, Greggory picked out bundles of notes wrapped with a single paper band sellotaped in the middle like a Christmas decoration. He removed each wad of notes from the bands and then one by one he placed the twenty-pound notes and the ten-pound notes under an ultraviolet lamp. Every 100th note in each batch was marked with a pen that could not be seen without the lamps glow. These notes had all been given code numbers. Greggory took each of these notes and placed them in a separate pile before sliding the remaining wad back into the paper hoop. Once this was done, he replaced the notes under the floorboards. There was a lot of money and the work strained his back and his eyes as he crouched over the desk. After several hours the job was done and sat on the small desk in his spare bedroom was £1,600 in marked notes. Greggory placed these in a brown envelope and sealed it. He kept the surgical gloves on and placed the brown envelope into a plastic shopping bag. Removing the gloves and the surgical mask he had worn throughout, Greggory went down to his car and put the money under the front passenger seat making sure no part of the bag could be seen from outside the car. He returned to place the £162,140 remaining cash back under the boards and the rug.

While Greggory was hiding the proceeds from the robbery Hans was sitting on Loolie's floral sofa with a large whiskey in a tumbler. Loolie was snuggled up to him and Hans had his arm across her shoulders. He had eaten his fill of lentil and pork rib soup with homemade crust bread with delicious butter. They had retired to the sofa and were now watching the evening news from the Pebble Mill studios. The bank robbery was the second item. Up popped the local news reporter Fred Hodson wearing a grey Macintosh coat and standing on the High Street in Bromsgrove with the bank behind him behind police tape. A small crowd of children were behind him, sitting on Chopper and Raleigh racing bikes. Shoppers nonchalantly walked past him, as if it was every day that the news was being made in the town. Yesterday's bank raid on the bank in Bromsgrove is believed to have netted over £200,000 and is the biggest robbery in the history of the town. The last person to rob a bank in the town was hanged in front of the Black Cross pub. Hodson paused to let this sink in with his audience. Sources close to the bank's workforce have said that the armed men broke in and terrified the staff and customers. The Police have refused to make a comment...

Loollie turned her head up to Hans, who looked down.

"I hope this was not you"

....but sources close to the investigation say this follows a spate of gangland robberies......

"No, it's not me this time Loolie." said Hans reassuringly. We have given up that nonsense now the church is fixed up and the library is staying open."

..... the police are no nearer catching the gang......

"I have only just found you Hans. I don't want to lose you," Loolie said with enough concern in her voice for Hans to start stroking her hair.

"I promise you it is all over now," said Hans.

....A burned out van was found less than a mile from the incident and this is believed to be involved ... As the reporter spoke, pictures showed the shell of the burned-out van being pulled up onto a flatbed truck with a police car in front of it. In the next pictures Hunter and Savage could be seen leaving the bank.

"Do you promise me Hans?"

Hunter was saying "No comment" to the reporter on the screen. He got into the car with Savage and the camera followed them as they drove away.

"I promise." said Hans "I have had enough excitement for one life."

The next morning Greggory drove to Solihull and parked round the corner from Big Reg's house. He got out dressed as a postman, a uniform he had hired in a fancy-dress shop in Yardley the weekend before. He walked round the corner and stopped outside the gates using the bag to cover any trace of his fingerprints. He squeezed the brown envelope from out of the bag directly into the red-letter box that sat on the garage gates before returning to the car and driving home. A man in a rumpled suit, tired from his four-hour surveillance, and annoyed that his replacement was already twenty minutes late, wrote onto a pad '07.21 postman'.

A different postman arrived outside Freddie's cottage that morning bringing a letter from the council. He paused under the roses that ringed the door. He knocked. Freddie opened the door.

"Morning sir," said the postman. "The roses smell fantastic; you have a parcel and a letter sir."

"Thank you," Freddie put the parcel on the table by the door. He was expecting a delivery of seeds. Freddie opened the letter in the hallway. It was from the Alms Houses Trustees. He stood in his striped pyjamas reading. He ran his hand through his hair.

"Well, I'll be," he said to himself. "That changes everything."

After delivering the envelope to Big Reg, Greggory toyed with the idea of visiting Lynn, a woman he enjoyed seeing on a mutually agreeable basis several times each week. Lynn liked dressing up and had insisted that Greggory turn up at her home dressed as a fireman on one occasion. But even though his desire for Lynn was aroused by wearing the postman's uniform and the memory of her enthusiastic love making, he decided to go straight home.

Peter's diary

I am awake too early, stiff and dehydrated, sometimes with my heart racing and one of, my arms empty of blood. I have to pump my hands to get the circulation going again. Then in either darkness or twilight I think of pornographic thoughts which stops me falling back to sleep. Then stuck in restlessness the day emerges and I feel disappointed that there is no adventure and my alcohol use has become ridiculous. Self-loathing and self-pity are never a good way to start the day so I switched on an audio book and could hear Marianne's voice. She was reading Hemingway's short stories. The story was called Indian Camp and Marianne read it in an American accent. What an extraordinarily kind and generous woman she is. When she had finished reading, I clambered out of my bed and showered. Decide that I should bake her scones as a thank you. Nothing else happened today.

Chapter Seventeen

Friday night for Big Reg was dog's night. He liked the dogs. He liked gambling and he liked to be seen flashing his wealth among the other punters who were a mix of ordinary working men and women who bet small and could never win big. For dog racing was a lottery. The Birmingham track was in Dudley, in the heart of the Black Country, near to the big brewery and was popular but for the small group of animal rights protesters who stood with placards with photos of dead dogs near the entrance. It was a small stadium.

Reg would arrive in his Jaguar and go straight to the owner's restaurant. He wasn't an owner of racing dogs but who was to stop him? He was 6 foot four and as wide as a doorway. When he lifted himself out of the driving seat of the car the Jaguar righted itself relieved from the dead weight of such a large man. The restaurant was above the start and finish line and looked down from a balcony to the cheaper restaurant with its chicken and chips Friday suppers. Below this was the paddock which was the other side of great window panes of the restaurant. Here, exposed to the elements stood the masses paying less than a couple of pounds for entry and served with hot Bovril, tins of beer and cheap burgers. Here also were the bookmakers stood next to their blackboards of chalk written odds with tickets in one hand and a roll of money in the other. When Reg took his table seat on the balcony, he looked around the room and then across the field and track. He did not notice the eight police officers who were hidden in plain sight. Reg did not bet on the first race; instead, he ordered two steaks and a bottle of champagne. A few minutes after he had taken his seat his ex-wife appeared dressed in a short-sleeved silver dress that hugged her shapely figure. She was a platinum blonde and she wore enough gold and diamonds to scream new money to any of the other punters who wanted to form an opinion of her.

"Are you feeling lucky tonight, Reg?" she purred.

"I am indeed Dotty. Did you pick up a card?"

The card, as Reg called it, was a booklet showing the races and times and also the form of the dogs over distances and different races. It allowed the punter to think that the racing and the betting was in some way a mathematical challenge. That a good clear mind could pick the winners. Of course, the card was a product of the twenty odd bookmakers that were licenced to the track. If Reg had ignored the card and bet his money on the dog running on the inside trap, he would have maybe lost less money over the years. But he didn't care. He bought into the illusion that he was an aficionado and expert gambler glorying in his winnings and forgetting the losses. At the end of the day, he said it's about the fun, the show and having sex with his ex-wife every Friday and then falling into a drunken sleep. As far as Dotty was concerned, she hoped he would fall asleep sooner rather than later for she would go through his pockets and remove a good portion of his cash. This was on top of the £800 he gave her every week at the dogs. It was a working relationship in her eyes.

After their steaks, which Dotty barely touched and Reg finished, he started to drink heavily, ordering Rum and Cokes and passing money to the bookies lads who would run the bets down on the bottom floor and out into the cold.

Each bet was made to the same bookie. Tadstows was the big money bookie and Reg liked to bet big making sure that when he handed over the money it could be seen by all around him. He would produce a roll of twenty-pound notes as thick as a navvy's wrists and slowly peel off the notes and hand them to the boy. The boy was actually probationary constable David Brownsword his first time in plain clothes and acting with a calm that hid his inexperience and his acute terror at being so close to a man he had read would torture and maim anyone who stood in his way. Brownsword had been chosen because he was the youngest looking officer on the force.

Tadstow was a long serving crook and the police had so much on him, frauds, thefts and debts, that he only achieved his licence each year because of the information he was prepared to hand over to the police. As his runner handed over the notes from Reg, he would turn and hand the notes to the plain clothes police man who would hand him back the same amount of money. The officer would then place the notes from Big Reg into his top jacket pocket. As the night moved on, these notes were processed outside by Savage, who sat in a van in the carpark with an ultraviolet lamp.

About half way through the evening the marked notes started to come through. Each one was placed in an evidence bag. Another officer sat beside Savage writing numbers on the top of the evidence bag before placing them in a cardboard box on the floor of the van.

"We've got him," said Savage.

*

Hunter was at home waiting for a call. He lived with his wife and two children in a 70's detached house in Redditch. The living room, where he sat, had all the trappings of a man doing well for himself. Colour TV and the latest video recorder. A Hitachi music centre sat on the sideboard next to a vase of red roses.

An electric carriage clock ticked away over an unlit gas fire. His wife brought him a mug of tea and some biscuits. He was sitting watching a Jacques Cousteau documentary when the phone rang at 10pm.

He lifted himself from the sofa, patting the head of the Labrador that lay at his feet next to him.

"Hello," he barked down the phone.

"It's me boss," panted Savage filled with excitement at the news he was about to divulge.

"Ok what have you got?" said Hunter, expecting some good news at the end of the week.

"We've got him sir. He used about a grand's worth of the notes from the bank. Smith is bagging and tagging them right now."

"A grand?"

"Yes boss. They have been coming in steadily over the last hour. The first lot was nothing and we were going to give up on it and call it a night. But then they started coming one after another."

"Great work Mike," said Hunter, calling Savage by his first name only happened when he was really pleased and he could almost feel the grin on Savage's face on the other end of the phone.

"Oh, and there is another thing?"

"Go on," said Hunter

"Forensics looked the van over."

"It was a burnt-out shell; they can't have got much. Please tell me if there was a fingerprint?"

"No boss, a little stranger than that. The explosion was caused by an acid detonator."

"What is that?"

"It's a simple timing device where acid eats through a membrane and sets off the fire. The size of the membrane determines when the fire would start. Clever. The forensics people said the bomb maker would have to have good knowledge to create this. They were used by SOE in the war, very rare bits of kit."

"The sort of thing a gangland leader would have access to?"

"Certainly boss."

"So, are we looking for old members of SOE?"

"Well, the Germans and Japanese used them as well sir." Savage was scratching his head.

"Not much use to me that Savage. But you did well on the money sting."

"Shall we bring him in, Boss?" Savage asked.

"No, Let's do some checks first then bring him in. He is a bit handy when he's had a few drinks. I don't want anyone getting hurt. We will get him early on Sunday. I will see you tomorrow."

"Goodnight, Boss."

The line went dead.

Hunter sat down on the sofa and wondered why all the marked notes had come out in one go when they had been spaced evenly in the bundles or so the report from the bank had said. He discarded this thought because he knew he had him, and in the inevitable trial that would follow they would only disclose part of the money evidence to ensure some crafty gangster lawyer did not ask that question too. Hunter knew how to play the game of justice. This was justice for this man and it was coming at long last.

Big Reg would have no alibi for his whereabouts on the afternoon of the bank robbery because he was doing something far worse at the time. He had had a rival kidnapped that morning and as the Allotment Gang were entering the bank Big Reg was peeling the toe nails off one of the other Birmingham crooks. Later he would be bagged and suffocated while Big Reg watched. The body was never found. A rumour was spread that he had gone to Spain to start a new life and after a few weeks the disappearance had been filed away with all the other missing persons. Justice, in its own peculiar way may be served after all.

*

On Monday at 6am seven police vehicles drove up to the house in Solihull. The gates were quickly pushed aside and six vehicles drove into the driveway crunching the gravel and skidding to a halt. Twelve officers got out of the vans and cars and four ran immediately around to the back of the house. Two officers began to ram open the door with a battering ram. The door sprang open after thirty seconds of vigorous work and eight policemen, some with shields and helmets like medieval knights charged into the house. Four went straight up the stairs and four searched the down stairs. Big Reg had been asleep, he was in a leaden drunken sleep his heart rate went from 70 to 140 beats a minute in less than twenty seconds from hearing the noise of the ram at his door. He rolled over and into a sitting position on the bed just as the thunder of heavy boots came up the stairs.

"Police!" Hunter shouted from the door.

At this moment the bedroom door flew open and before Big Reg could stand, he was pinned to the bed by the shields of two enormous policemen. The police were not taking any chances with Big Reg's fearsome reputation for fighting arresting officers. Two other police officers arrived and spun the large man onto his back and he was cuffed quickly and then the shields pressed him back down onto the bed because even handcuffed Big Reg could do a lot of physical damage.

His girlfriend was in the bed with him when the officers had crashed in and was screaming loudly as Big Reg was pinned down. She jumped out of the bed as the officers had dived on him and stood naked next to the wardrobe.

"Fabulous Knockers," sneered the officer in full riot gear standing at the bedroom door.

"I'll get you for that you nonce." Big Reg said, muffled by the two officers and shields that lay across him. He struggled and heaved some more but the two policemen were his match in size and weight.

"Shut up," said Savage to the policeman, throwing the woman a dressing gown. "We don't need him wound up any more than he already is." She put on the dressing gown and spat at the officer. She was now robed in a silk kimono, her blonde hair like a bird's nest and bright red lipstick smeared from her lips across her cheeks, black lines of tear-stained mascara ran down to meet the lipstick smear. Even in this dishevelled state Savage thought she still managed to look fabulous.

"Cut it out love or we will take you in with this wanker," said the policeman lying on top of a heavy shield pining Big Reg's legs. A police woman stepped forward and led the crying woman into another room.

"Come on my lovely, let's get you a cup of tea," she said.

Hunter marched in through the front door nodding at the four policemen who had searched the downstairs.

"Good work lads," he said.

"Up here Boss!" Came the shout from above and Hunter ran up the stairs to read the rights.

Reg was sat up on the bed wrapped in a sheet and appeared to have calmed down though he eyed the officer who had made the comment about his ex-wife and was mentally storing his face and badge number in his mind. Reg was never one not to harbour a grudge. As Reg was being placed in the back of the van, still naked but wrapped in a sheet, PC Smith sidled up to Hunter with a box containing a CB radio set.

"It's still in the box sir. Doesn't look like it's been opened, never mind used," said the young constable.

"Thank you, son. But we are the detectives here," said Hunter. He looked at the box. The cellophane had been partially removed from the box but he was right, it did not look opened. He handed the box to Savage.

"Rough up the box a little," he said "and make sure it bloody works before you put it in an evidence bag."

"Sir," acknowledged Savage, taking the unused CB radio out to the waiting police car.

*

Griffin sat alone in his study with the freshly made contract on the large desk before him. The chair he sat on was Georgian but the desk was a great Victorian campaign desk that had once been owned by his hero Cecil Rhodes. Like him he had become a millionaire at 18 years old. He had become rich through hard work and cunning. He was an adventurer in business, and yet he believed he remained a man of simple pleasures and desires. He had grown up in the 60s on a Merseyside council estate. There was no inheritance and no fancy schooling or University. Only a few of his friends in the business world came from nothing. Money is inherited to the elite like poverty is inherited from the poor. He had done well because he knew when he could win and he knew when he was beaten. His motto had always been 'Next'.

Move forward. never look back. Do not hold grudges. They impair judgement. So what? He was to lose a small plot of land in a shabby little allotment. He would still make over £80,000 on the house he had bought just a few years ago. London called. London was calling him back. Griffin fiddled with the gold fountain pen in his hand. He read the contract again, never knowingly trusting even the lawyers that worked for him. He had known that he was likely to be honoured by the Queen and given a knighthood at New Year. The speculation was created by his own endeavours. He had made the necessary substantial gift to the Party and made it known at functions that he expected a return on his donation. He had some newspaper friends who he urged to make comments on his altruism and good deeds. He had toyed with the idea of buying the Alms Houses that were in trouble and gifting them to the community, but he realised the money would be better served serving himself and the party he loved. It was just a question of time for the letter to arrive from the Queen's household stating that her majesty was minded to offer a knighthood and he would, humbly, accept. The only problem he faced was the arrow embedded in his front door which arrived with a thud. The target was a brown envelope and inside was a proposition and some photographs. The proposition was a simple one. To remove the allotment clause from his deeds and free up the allotment he had so enjoyed these past two summers of retirement. It was a simple business but it was still the blackmail business. The photos were taken inside his shed, though how, he did not know. When he had gone to the shed that morning there was no camera at the angle shown in the photos. He wondered why this would be an issue, such a trivial issue of ownership. The blackmailer must be one of the other men he had upset on the site. But after the unpleasantness with the punch and his brother-in-law turning up in a show of solidarity and strength nothing had occurred. He had carried on as if nothing had happened. It must be one of them he mused.

But, changing the deed when he was already considering a move back to his house in Holland Park was no big thing, especially if he was to get the gong from the queen. Once he was awarded, they never took them back. They gave them out to arms dealers and the like; several sirs had even gone to jail even. He had done no wrong to anyone and what if he did like the ladies, he thought, as he signed his name on the deal. There was no time to quibble, the world was going to the dogs and even his beloved prime minister had nearly lost her life in a Brighton hotel. The bloody IRA had missed only because she was working late and not in her bed like most people. Hard work had saved her and hard work was going to get him his knighthood and the recognition he deserved.

Peter's diary

Tonight, I was at the allotment working in the dark, my dark and everyone else's dark. I could hear the hoot of an owl coming from the woods. The owl is the sound of the night and the foreshadow of death in folk lore. I thought I was alone with the fecund smell of the soil. It was cool not cold and autumn was near. Just round the corner. I was not alone, Freddie was pottering about until late. I think he has a show tomorrow and he was preparing some huge vegetables for display. I could hear his footsteps clearly. Freddie moved with style. He made small steps when he was working but when he left the allotment, he took large strides. Freddie whistles a lot too. I could hear him earlier repeating an old song. I could not remember the song title but it was a jolly sound. Later Freddie came towards me and without mincing his words he said "I think you know what has been going on and the state that Tom has got himself in" I nodded "we would appreciate it if you didn't mention this. It was all for the good of the community but has got a little out of hand he said. When I told him that I felt a little aggrieved that I had not been included, he slapped me on the back and said "goodman". He said he wanted to make a proposition to me. I was all ears, perhaps being all ears was the only help I could give. Then he told me an extraordinary thing. The council had stepped in and purchased the alms houses and therefore the money from the bank robbery, which was intended to use to buy them, was now no longer needed. Freddie said that we were literally standing over £160,000 cash buried here in the allotment when I said the newspapers said it was £200,000, he said that was just paper talk. He wanted Rosie and I to give the money away. To spend the next two years stuffing cash into envelopes and giving it to charities all across the area. I would be spending the next few years literally giving money away. You would make a lot of people happy, he said. Rosie had already said yes. Greggory has spoken with her earlier. I consented and with that I joined the Allotment Gang. After years of leading this life of darkness I feel that a ray of light has touched me and given me purpose again.

Chapter Eighteen

Little Stoke had seen history and had let history pass it by. All the great moments: the Roman, Viking and Norman invasions, the civil war, the German bombing and even the Domesday survey had been and gone and left no trace of the village. The village itself-had no need to have grown here, it was not a strategic site, it had no castle or even a defensive structure, no barrows for burial, no stone circles. It was sat at no crossroads or on a major route or road, it did not contain a pilgrimage trail or even a priory, nunnery or monastery, apart from the church. It was not the place of a major river crossing. The canal and railway building manias had not deemed the village important enough for either to pass through. The motorway and railway were within five miles but they joined two more important and celebrated places. Little Stoke had no coal or even the salt of nearby Droitwitch, or the romance of the building of a French princess's château in the Worcestershire sunshine. Even the new town of Redditch had better shops and facilities. In short nothing had put Little Stoke onto the map. Yet there were a few Elizabethan houses, a few rows of Victorian homes and a high street consisting of two public houses, a butcher, grocers', bakery, the library a food store and Marco's café. The village with its mixture of thatched and slate roofs had developed around farming and farm labourers. Then it became a commuter village for the bigger towns and nearby Birmingham. House prices had risen steadily to the point in the early 1980s that few young people could afford to buy a home here. And older people complained about the prices in the pubs and the cost of living in general.

'Billys' was the narrow blue shop front in the centre of the village. The shop was as wide as a single window and doorway and was squeezed between the butchers and the newsagents. It had a traditional red and white swirling pole outside and the interior looked unchanged since the 1950s when Billy had moved in and set up a business. There were two heavy leather and chrome chairs, with one always empty and unused and a bench behind for those waiting to be barbered. Various newspapers were cast along the bench of red leather that made a squeak when you moved on it. A coat stand stood in one corner next to the bench with an umbrella and a spare barber's jacket hanging from it. The room was painted in a dark blue with a white ceiling. There were posters for cruise ships on the back wall and various black and white photos of Billy with various women in Havana or New York. Billy had been a barber on the Cunard liners and was well travelled. He had cut the hair of many famous politicians, writers and even film stars who travelled from New York on business or to Cuba for vacations. Around the two mirrors and sinks there were postcards from all over the world, mainly because Billy collected stamps and his customers would always send him a card when they were visiting a different country on holiday or at work. There were shelves filled with all sorts of tonics and Billy still sold condoms. Billy stood tall in black trousers and a white barber's jacket. He had worn a small white hat for years but had recently discarded it when someone said he looked like a servant rather than a barber. Billy was subservient to no one. Inside the breast pocket various steel combs and scissors peeked. Billy had extraordinary, luscious and quaffed hair. Swept back all shades of grey. His fingernails were perfect and he took great pride in his appearance. At the age of 68 he had fought on against age and kept his working life going.

He liked people and he could not face retirement alone in his house with his ailing wife. Work defined a man he thought and he enjoyed being around people. Billy was the font of all knowledge in the village, anything from a current planning application, a divorce, a scandal, to a new business starting up, he knew about it all. To give up the business and the company of people was more than he could bear. He did not need the money he earned since he had paid off his mortgage some years ago. He just enjoyed his work. Coming to a job you love doing is not a job he would say.

Billy had cut the hair of only two men that morning. One had been one of the local characters Brendan Suckling who owned the food store at the start of the village. A man who also hovered over his customers waiting for them to make choices, especially children on the way to school who he believed were always trying to shoplift sweets from him. The second customer had been Stanley Eaves, the primary school teacher, who had been known by everyone in the village as the Colonel. The colonel was not or ever had been a Colonel but had been a pilot sergeant in the RAF. He had crash landed his Hurricane in Yugoslavia during the war and spent the next two years fighting with Tito's guerrilla army. He was known as a strict schoolteacher and was enormously respected around the village. He had taught almost everyone who lived in Little Stoke under the age of 40. He was a large man who rarely got out of his chair in lessons. He would arrive at school in the morning and chalk the notes he wanted the students to copy onto a modern rolling black board. While the children copied, he would read the newspaper or mark books. The Colonel had been on form and liked to tell funny stories and jokes. Like the rest of the village, he came for a cheap haircut, but also to find out what was going on in the village.

When Tom pushed open the door to the shop to the clattering sound of the doorbell Billy was sat in the spare chair reading the sports pages and whistling contently to himself.

"Someone is happy," said Tom.

"I'm always happy. It's like a curse" Billy said.

"Or it's a sign of a simpleton." Replied Tom as he sat down in the big chair and stared at himself in the mirror. Billy smiled. Tom smiled back raising his eyes to signify that he needed a haircut and Billy was to get on with it. Tom and Billy had been friends since school. They were the only boys in their class who had gone onto college education and at one point they were the only ones who had shoes.

"How would you like your haircut today, Tom?"

"In silence," Tom grinned. He could see himself in the mirror and wondered when he had last smiled.

Billy threw a striped sheet around Tom and fastened it round his neck, then tore off a paper towel and pushed this between the sheet and the back of Tom's neck. Tom immediately noticed how good Billy smelled.

"You smell good today, Billy."

"Don't tell me ...Like a whores handbag Tom?"

Billy began to comb Tom's hair back and lifted the longer strands pinning little tufts between his thumb and fingers. The scissors snapped across the strands. Billy launched into his chat which Tom heard as background noise.

"There was trouble in the pub on Thursday, that mad bugger Felix. You know Bert's boy from the farm. He was having a row with his girlfriend and someone came and told him what for and got a thick ear. He's been barred for a month and good riddance. Such a good family, but he is a bloody hot head," Billy carried on about a lost cow, graffiti posted on the wall of the school.

Tom became quickly lost in his own thoughts as Barry chatted oblivious to Tom's silence. Rosie was now involved and she and Freddie were to get rid of the money. They were all putting each other in danger and it would not be long before they were all caught. It was a good idea to make a clean break between those who had committed the robberies and those who handed out the money. He had left Rosie and Peter filling envelopes with cash and labelling addresses from the list of those who received food gifts from the church harvest festival. They had decided to put £200 in each envelope. Tom had watched them through the shed window. Envelopes on one side of the potting table and money on the other. Leave it for a year he had told them. Let the whole thing go cold. But let's just get a bit of cash to those who needed it right now.

"So, the lad was in more trouble because he's taken money from his mother who had been given a gift from an old friend." Billy continued in a stream of consciousness.

Tom started to think of his oldest friend and had to dismiss the thought from his head because he did not wish to practice self-pity. But dismissing a thought is not as easy as he had used to find it. His wife had been so pretty when they had met. He had been too frightened to ask her on a date. She would never say yes to an ordinary man like me he had thought. He had seen her in the local pub and occasionally at the Rex Picture House. They knew of each other, but had not spoken.

"Still no news on the Bank robbery in Bromsgrove." said Billy.

He had to wait until he got on a bus on a dark winter day, sometime in 1947 and could see her sitting on the first seat. She had smiled recognising him, so he had gone and sat next to her. They had got off at the same stop and he had plucked up the courage to ask her to have tea and cake with him.

"The police are useless; they have not got a clue what's going on." Said Billy.

They had found a little cake shop and had sat chatting on a big green leather sofa and a snack that should have taken half an hour had kept them for two hours. His nerves had gone even though he was talking ten to the dozen. She had calmed him by saying that he was trying too hard. He smiled at the way she had the ability to keep him calm and in a good place even from that first meeting.

"I bet if you were to park for a second on a double yellow, they would be down on you like a shot." Said Billy.

Before he left for the cinema, a few days after meeting on the bus, he had to change his clothes twice because he wanted to make an impression. He had opted for a casual jacket shirt and tie. He had been issued with a demob suit but he had been a lot thinner when he was issued it. She had turned up in a summer floral dress which was very fashionable in the late forties. She was wearing thick red lipstick and had put her hair up in a bun under a scarf. He knew the moment he saw her that he wanted to spend the rest of his life with her.

"The colonel thinks it's a gang from Birmingham. It was all so professional." said Billy.

The problem was that he had outlived her. He had always presumed that he would be the first to pass. He's picked up malaria in Burma and it had made him thin and weak for many years. She had joked about getting a dog to replace him when he died. Tom did not like dogs. I shall call it Little Tom she joked.

"They were in and out like the SAS. A proper little unit just like the Iranian embassy lot." said Billy.

Marriage did follow and so did a happy life. He looked at his face in the mirror with Billy standing behind him snipping and talking. He could not stop thinking about her. She would be cross that he had taken so many risks and that he had pulled so many people into this dangerous circle of events. If she had been here, he would have something to lose but now he didn't feel he had anything to lose but his soul.

"And the Colonel knows about these things as you well know." said Billy

Tom looked up at Billy in the mirror.

"What is the country coming to Billy?" said Tom.

"To hell on a handcart." replied Billy.

Tom had made up his mind. He wanted no more of the thefts. There was just too much danger for all of them. It could not go on and he felt that for his sake justice needed to be served. Billy removed the sheet from across his shoulders and began to sweep his clothes with a brush.

"Anything for the weekend sir?" said Billy.

Chapter Nineteen

Autumn came in slowly, as it does. Creeping along, mixing sunshine and rain, warm days and cold. Then, too early, frost and bright blue skied sunny mornings. The Allotment Gang were met each day by barren early morning frosts that stripped the trees bare in just a few days. The frosts had come hard this year. The leaves, all golden, lay on the floor, frozen before they could rot into the earth or be swept up and placed in the composting bins. Crows cawed in the woods and the allotment looked bare but for the angular shapes of the buildings. Colour was lost to the eye, as the land took on the feel of an old black and white movie. There was no buzz of insects, just a hand-wringing cold, that pushed through the layers of clothes and got into the bones. The soil was frozen into clumps in the raised beds. A nose would pick up no scents and even the pungent smell of composting could not be detected. Yet the land still retained a striking beauty. For some, the emergence of winter was their favourite time of the year. For others, the dark days and long nights brought on winter depressions and anxiety. There would be a long wait to be able to turn their faces up to the spring sunshine. Darkness would reign for a while yet. The onset of the cold and the dark had affected Tom more than usual. Tom was becoming consumed with guilt at what he had done. That he had enjoyed the excitement of the planning and the execution of three armed robberies made him feel worse. He had always known he would go to heaven when he died, and there he would be reunited with his wife. But his Christian faith did not mix well with his recent actions. During the war he had seen and done some shocking things and he thought that the lack of choice and the Christian doctrine of forgiveness would see him through those wicked times. He had known real fear in his life. That time during Operation White City, when he had been split from his Chindit column and spent three days lying in his own faeces, while Japanese soldiers searched for British stragglers to torture and kill. That was fear. Pure unadulterated fear. Grinding in its nature and never forgotten in all these years. But now he was fearful of betraying his God and his political philosophy. Of mistaking a good deed as something that was born out of threats of violence and theft. He had lived his life well. He had been guided by a personal philosophy that had allowed him to conduct himself with quietness and dignity. Generosity in all things and to all people, active service to others, a belief in community and simple justice and fairness in all his dealings. Love at the heart of all relationships, kindness and decency. This way of living had helped dispel the tragedy of his youth. Putting right the indignity of war and living a good life to pay for the lives of the friends who he had lost. But also, to attempt to amend for the three lives he had taken. The Japanese soldier who had woken from a slumber next to a Burmese river, who he had dragged into the water and drowned with the same hands he stared at now. He had nightmares about this man. The other two had been in a truck which he shot with a Piat anti-tank round in the western desert. The driver killed instantly and the other burned, trapped in the wreck of the vehicle. A true horror show. Having been a killer in his youth he was now a thief at the end of his life. As Tom thought before the fireplace of logs and coal, he became overwhelmed with grief for his wife and his lost soul. What would she have said and done?

*

The Armistice ceremony started at 10.30 the next morning. Hans had arrived first with a gift for Tom. It was a box of medals.

"Put them on," he said, "you earned them."

"I threw mine away at the end of the war Hans. You don't wear yours for the same reason."

"Actually, I don't wear mine because the people of the village don't want to see an ex German paratrooper wearing a Knights Cross and the Iron cross when they commemorate the dead of two wars against my old country."

"Here," he pushed the box towards Tom.

"How did you get these?"

"I bought them from an antiques and medal shop in the Bull Ring. I am afraid they are all genuine except the big one. I had to get a copy of that Tom. They tend to be a little expensive these days."

"I have never worn them before. I never needed a badge for doing the dreadful things I have had to do.

"If you are going to give yourself up then at least go in style."

"How do you know I am going to give myself up?"

"We have known for a while Tom. We discussed it and decided that we would not do the same. I don't want to see out my last few years surrounded by villains in some shocking prison cell smelling of shit and piss. Plus, I have other people to consider now." He smiled.

"So, if you feel that this is what you want to do, we will not try and stop you. I know you too well for that. Just remember the rest of us are a group of silly old men who work an allotment. No names, hey?"

"No names." said Tom.

*

Tom pinned the sizable rack of medals onto his coat.

"Let's go, I want to be there on time."

The two old men marched from Tom's house down the road with beech trees dripping water from the bare branches. There were no leaves because the early frosts had meant the trees had shed the golds and browns onto the pavement. Half way down the tunnel of beech Freddie joined them dressed in a long black coat and boots with such a shine on them, you could see the houses reflected on the tips as they walked towards the cenotaph.

Greggory was already there, standing near the guides, scouts and cubs. He held a wreath of poppies that he had made using fresh poppies from the fields of Flanders. He ordered them every year and the large Dutch man who drove the flowers across Europe to deliver to all the flower shops in the county had made a special trip to get them. Greggory had made the wreath the night before. It was paid for by all the Allotment Gang members.

*

A collection of boys wearing the uniform and beret of the Worcestershire's stood in three rows at ease. Major Bennett, who had led a brigade of the Worcestershire's in World War 2, stood at the end of the row. As did the Colonel, who was in charge of the local TA, but had been a flight Sergeant in World War 2 and had crashed his Hurricane into Yugoslavia and had joined Tito's men for the duration of the war. He was only ever referred to as The Colonel, never by his name.

A crowd of people stood around the Cenotaph leaving a space for the cadets and old soldiers to march through and lay their wreaths.

"Morning Greggory," Freddie said as they approached a very smart man sporting the George Cross, a solitary medal on his chest for the British government had still not seen fit to create a medal for the merchant men who had risked life every day of the war.

Greggory turned and looked at the Allotment Gang.

Hans said: "It has been decided."

"No names?" said Greggory towards Tom.

"No names," returned Tom.

Across the road from the Cenotaph square, in a car with a clear view of the ceremony, sat George Keates, late of the 8th Army, and his grandson Stephen. George was a very thin man, short in stature. He had wet down what little hair he had with pomade, and combed it back over his head. His face was not lined with age, but his eyes were heavily sunken into his thin face. He was wearing a green cardigan with grey trousers. A poppy on his chest. His grandson Stephen was in a red track suit and wore his hair long. He had the round puppy fat face of an eight-year-old.

"Shall we get out of the car, grandad?" Stephen asked.

"No. It looks like it's going to throw it down and we didn't bring coats. And your mother will kill me if I bring you home soaked. We can watch from here."

"He has a lot of medals," said the little boy.

"Which one?" replied George.

"That one with the bowler hat on."

"What are they for grandad?"

"Oh, he must have been a very brave man because he is wearing an MC."

'What's an MC?'

"It's the Military Cross. Just one down from the Victoria Cross. That is a very rare medal. They only give those to very brave men and women."

"What about all the others he's wearing?"

"They are campaign and service medals. The star shaped medal shows he was in Burma. The forgotten army they were called. Every army had a name in those days. We were called the D-Day dodgers because we were fighting in Italy."

"That's a bit rude isn't it granddad? To call soldiers fighting a war, dodgers."

"It was said by some silly politician and we wore it as a badge of honour and even had a song about it. We all sang it; we took pride in being in Italy." George began to sing in a trembling baritone.

"We are the D-Day Dodgers

Out in Italy,

Always on the vino,

Always on the spree.

Eighth Army skivers and their tanks,

We go to war in ties like swanks.

For we are the D-Day Dodgers,

In sunny Italy."

"Do you know I am surprised to remember the words. I have not sung that for over 40 years." said George.

"That sounds funny grandad. Were you on the vino?" he said innocently.

"Cheeky!" George leant across the car and tickled Stephen who giggled loudly.

"Did it make you angry then grandad?"

"Oh, we were really cross about it. You see we fought all the way across North Africa and at the end we thought we would go home and give someone else a chance to be a hero. But the big man at the top wanted experienced troops so we had to invade Italy."

"Do you have many medals grandad?"

"I did not accept them. Many of us refused to pick them up. We did our duty and that was enough. I did not want a medal for doing what had to be done."

"You should wear your medals grandad."

"I don't think you will ever understand Stephen." George paused and then realising he's probably hurt his grandson's feelings said, "Do you see the black fella with the wreath? The one with just one medal?"

"Yes," said Stephen

"That is a big medal, son. It's the George Cross. It was given to civilians as the highest medal for bravery."

"So, he wasn't a soldier like you, grandad?"

"No, that is Greggory. He was a merchant sailor. A very brave man indeed."

"In the Royal Navy?"

"No, a merchant sailor works on cargo ships. They brought the food and the guns and tanks from America. Without their work we would have starved and probably lost the war. Now shush look, it's about to start."

The Reverend James led a procession from the church out into the square. Behind him choir boys followed and behind them a few men and women dressed smartly in dark suits. Several of them carried wreaths, a police officer and two of the local magistrates and a collection of councillors, one wearing a white poppy completed the procession. Reverend James arrived at the lectern dressed in his cassock and began to read the service. He talked of sacrifice and the fight against fascism. How the world was a far better place because of the actions of men and women in two World Wars. He talked of the lessons to be learned from war and that we should strive for peace at every opportunity. He talked of the recent war in the Falklands and how Britain must endeavour to hold firm in the fight against tyranny, wherever it raises its head in the world. He spoke of the men of peace and the political prisoners around the world and how important the fight is for freedom, especially in South Africa. It was an uplifting speech for the Reverend had a way with words. They all sang Jerusalem and one of the altar boys read a poem by Rupert Brooke. The last post was played haltingly as little William Bowen was overtaken by nerves at the high notes. No one minded. The local brass band took up a jaunty version of It's a long way to Tipperary and the wreaths were laid with all the dignity and devotion that was required of the occasion. The Lord's prayer was recited by an audience that had swollen to several hundred. Then it was over for another year.

"Pub?" said Freddie

"Pub." Came the reply from a group of the most unlikely gangsters.

Just going to have a word with George first said Freddie. Freddie crossed to speak to George in his car.

"Morning George," he said. Is this young Stephen?"

Stephen smiled his answer.

*

"Just to let you know that at long last we have a vacancy on the allotments and your name came up as top of the list. I was asked by the committee to see if you still wanted it. I can pop the contract round tomorrow if you'd like?"

"Freddie, that's great news. I will come over tomorrow and sign on." At this George started the engine of the Hillman and drove off home.

They stood in the saloon bar surrounded by old soldiers, sailors and airmen. Different hats and berets were resplendent on heads. Two Paras with red berets, still young men from the Falklands war, talked to Hans about the Battle of Goose Green. One already showing signs of post-traumatic stress disorder in his speech and an anxious demeanour. Across the room sat the Colonel surrounded by cadets and serving soldiers who he had taught over the years in the local school. Mrs Silverman, the landlady, served roasted chicken and gravy sandwiches, and the old stories poured out for a few hours until she called time at 2pm for the opening hours still met with wartime Sunday restrictions even in 1985.

Tom went out in the rain to the allotment, still in his suit and medals. Here he found a bottle of whiskey and started to drink. Freddie and Greggory joined him.

Across the village Savage and Hunter were meeting with the local sergeant to ensure that Big Reg's conviction would be secured. They were all in uniform because they had attended a different Remembrance parade earlier in the day and had yet to change. Savage and Hunter were trying to encourage the sergeant to amend bits of his evidence.

"You see Brian," said Hunter to the sergeant "policemen are like historians. They look at the evidence and create a story joining up the facts like a dot-to-dot picture. The problem for policemen and historians is just the same too. Sometimes the dots are far apart meaning the facts don't quite fit the story that needs to be told. In these circumstances we need to ensure that the story is respected by a jury. The dots have to join up to make the perfect picture."

"Where are we going with this?" questioned the sergeant. He was long enough in the career to know exactly where this was going.

"The problem we have is that we want to link Big Reg to the other little robberies. Make the link that he craved and needed excitement and would brag about it on CB radio. But we have a little problem. Reg is not called big Reg for nothing."

At this Savage flicked open his notebook and began to describe the robbers at the petrol station. "Three men, one small 5ft 5 and skinny like a teenager, the second of average build 5ft 9 walked with a slight limp, the third tall maybe 6ft 1 but also very thin."

"None of these descriptions matches a 6ft 4 colossus of a man called, lovingly, Big Reg. The jury will take one look at this fella sat in the dock and say he is not part of this gang even though we have a transcript of him bragging about night duties at a service station and a nice little earner."

It does not fit and if there is doubt the jury will not convict him. That is how it works. And then, this murdering bastard walks free and carries on his criminal and nefarious activities."

"What do you want from me?" said the sergeant.

"Well, you did the interviews along with Savage here. We just need to change the transcript so that one of them meets the description. Now young Savage here realises the importance of good policing and good policing is measured by convictions, not by giving a kid a thick ear for scrumping damsons."

"That's right boss," said Savage rather unconvincingly.

Hunter lent in towards the sergeant and said: "Come on Brian. You know how this works just like I do."

The station doorbell rang. It was a slight relief for the sergeant because Hunter had terrible breath and he had been breathing through his mouth, it was all he could do to avoid gagging.

"Let me get this. It may be important," the sergeant said and lifted the counter door and went to the door of the station. Savage and Hunter exchanged glances as the door was opened. There stood a very wet Tom. The rain dripped off his cap. His thick coat was bedecked with medals. A white shirt and suit and tie soaked through as if Tom had walked around the village all afternoon in the rain.

"Hello Tom. What brings you here?" Tom, dripping wet, stepped into the warm of the police station and the bright light of the admissions room.

Savage and Hunter turned to see an old man, wet through and in a state of inebriation. They cast an expert eye over the drunk. Tom, his face creased with wrinkles and wearing thick spectacles hiding rheumy eyes red from the tears and frustrations of over thinking everything that had happened. He was drunk but was also in a state of mental exhaustion and self-loathing.

"Tom have you been drinking?" said the sergeant.

"I will get straight to the point Brian," said Tom. "I have come to make a confession."

"A confession" said the sergeant incredulously.

"I have come to confess to the recent robberies."

Savage nudged Hunter with his elbow and they both stood up straight and turned away from the counter like two bar flies about to watch a fight.

"It was me I organised the robberies." Tom spluttered.

"You have been drinking Tom. Why don't you come back tomorrow and we can have a chat over a nice cup of tea?"

"No, sergeant, you have to arrest me because I am responsible for the robberies." Savage grinning stepped forward and said: "Are you ok, old fella?"

"Who are you?" said Tom.

"I am the officer," Savage paused "Er, we are the officers investigating the robberies."

"So, this is perfect timing," slurred Tom. "It was me." He said through whiskey breath. Tom wobbled like he was about to pass out. Hunter stepped forward and helped Tom to a waiting chair. Taking him gently by the arm and delivering him to the chair with a rare look of kindness in his eyes.

"Fine set of medals that mate. My grandad was in Burma too." Hunter said, noticing the Burma star. But he did not have as many as you have, old man. Looks like you are a bloody war hero. Is that an MC? Now, why would an old soldier like you want to rob the good people of Worcestershire?"

"I don't know," said Tom. "It was a bit of madness. I lost my moral compass and now I am here to confess my sins."

"You have come to the wrong place to confess your sins. So, you are saying that you are the leader of the crack group of villains who raided a petrol station, a post office and then pulled off one of the most audacious bank robberies in recent history? What is your name? How old are you?"

"My name is Tom and age is just a number. Age is a state of mind."

"No, it is not Tom," said Hunter. "Age is about losing your marbles and your abilities, it's going for a pee five times a night, it's about not being able to walk without a stick or a frame. It's about wheelchairs, nappies and nurses and doctors and care homes. It is about being sat all day in a chair watching television and dribbling from the side of your mouth. It is not about stealing cars, running into petrol stations and banks and waving guns around. That's a young man's game. And from where I am standing Tom you are not a young man."

"Who are the other three in your gang? Was it Billy the Kid and Wild Bill Hickock? Did you find them at the Crown Green bowling Club? Or was it at the Church Bring and Buy?" Said Savage with enough cutting sarcasm in his voice to fell a tree.

"Steady on," said the Sergeant to Savage "He's an old boy. Well respected in the village."

Savage said: "What did you do with the money old fella?"

"I can't tell you that," replied Tom

"Did you squander it on wine, women and song?" Savage said muffling a giggle.

"A fine Margeaux, and a bit of Vera Lynn," said Hunter. The Sergeant smiled and Savage snorted and grinned at the bad joke.

"Something like that." Tom replied, dropping his chin onto his chest. This was not going as well as he had expected. A thought crossed his mind that it was going better than expected for his confession had been made, ignored and now he would be seen to be exonerated before the law of the land.

"So, if you are the OAP war hero gangster, then can you explain how we have the actual gangster arrested and currently in a cell at Her Majesty's pleasure in HMP Balsall Heath awaiting trial?" said Hunter leaning back still basking in the current glory that surrounded him. For he had recently been told that his work on the case was a magnificent piece of detective work and he should expect a promotion in the near future. The Chief Constable had personally invited him into his office and had said officers like him had been overlooked for far too long, officers that moved with the times and could be relied upon to get the job done. Hunter had left the Chief Constable's office with a spring in his step and the thought of affording a foreign holiday once a year until he retired.

"What?" Tom slurred.

"Yes, old chap, we caught the leader of the gang weeks ago. He is rotting on remand as we speak."

"So, if we have the leader, what was your part? Were you just the hired gun?" Savage grinned a disbelieving grin as Hunter continued to dissect the story.

"There is no mention of a man your size with medals clinking on his chest."

"Well, there was but now there isn't." Savage said and the three policemen sniggered.

"You are not taking me seriously," said Tom "I have done a terrible thing. I wanted to be a good man and then something went wrong in my head and all this nonsense started."

"The only thing that went wrong here was a bit too much of the drink tonight and you decided to play silly buggers with the police," said the sergeant.

"Tom," continued the sergeant, "you are a pillar of the community. A God-fearing church going man. You raise money for charity, you garden those allotments and give food to the needy. A good man you are Tom, and armed robber you are not."

Hunter and Savage shook their heads. Savage tapped his watch and Hunter nodded back. They just wanted to get home and rescue what little was left of the weekend ahead of another fresh case that would inevitably land on their desk in the morning.

"I only ever wanted to be a good man," said Tom through whiskey breath, his lip quivering as the emotion and the drink returned to him. He reached into his pocket and pulled out a whiskey bottle.

"Will you join me officers?"

"No, we bloody well will not." Savage said impatiently and took the whiskey bottle from Tom and placed it on the floor by his feet. Tom picked it up and put it back in his pocket.

"Look grandad, I think the only thing you are guilty of is getting roaringly drunk all day with your old soldier buddies and playing silly buggers with us on your way home. And that's where you're going right now," said Hunter as he and Savage lifted Tom from his chair and directed him to the door.

"Sarge, does he have far to go?" Savage asked.

"No, he just lives round the corner."

"Shall we drop you off grandad. We were just leaving, that's if the good sergeant here makes the decision we want to hear." Hunter enquired.

"Ok, take him home. And yes, it is fine by me." said the sergeant. Joining up the dots was as easy as that. He had been too long on the force to know when justice needed a nudge in the right direction. He knew how to play the game and he knew that all vicious criminals had to have their day. And today was Big Reg's day. What's a little change in height and sizes? The witness was probably too scared at the time to get anything right. A confident witness is not always a good or accurate witness. He had been told that in training thirty-five years before by a court clerk.

"Send through the new transcript signed tomorrow. Thanks for your support, Brian." Tom looked bewildered by what the conversation was about. He was fuddled with whiskey and was starting to feel a bit sickly with it all.

"Come on Grandad let's get you in the car." Savage intoned in a gentler manner.

"It's ok, I will walk." said Tom. He did not want the neighbours to see him brought home a drunkard by the police especially now that being a professional gangster was no longer an option for the community to judge him by.

The Sergeant said: "For Christ's sake Tom, you are on the Parish Council. Get a grip on yourself man. I will not mention this, and I suggest you don't either. Goodnight."

The door was closed in a disgruntled fashion and Tom was left to the ignominious walk home with the harsh words of the sergeant ringing in his ears.

Tom staggered out into the rain with Hunter and Savage. They got in the police car parked on the drive of the little police station. Hunter wound the window down and said: "Safe journey old man. Got to be impressed by the way you have lived your life."

Tom grunted back. Hunter turned to Savage and said: "I hope when I am that old, I can still go out on a bender with my mates and end up confessing to robberies in a police station. It is the stuff of dreams. What a silly old sod."

They laughed as they drove off leaving Tom standing in the pouring rain, a free man, a good man, a man still wracked with god fearing guilt. But still free to walk home, and in the morning, he would shake off his hangover and dig over the potato beds with the rest of the Allotment Gang. As he walked past the church, he looked up to see the rain bouncing off the newly tiled roof. He stopped, pulled out the last of the whiskey and lent into the stone wall to steady himself. Tom lifted his face to the rain and shouted out the words of Albert Camus "In the midst of hate, I found there was, within me, an invincible love. In the midst of tears, I found there was within me, an invincible smile. In the midst of chaos, I found there was within me an invincible calm." The door of the church opened, sending a shaft of angular light across the graveyard and down the path piercing the rain that fell now in sheets. Silhouetted against the light in the doorway was Reverend James. James beckoned Tom toward the door.

The End

About the book

It is the 1980s. A group of elderly friends, connected by their love of their allotments (in Chaddersley Corbett!) are disgusted to discover that their, and other ordinary folks, pleasures and livelihoods are threatened by the rich and greedy. An unlikely 'gang', they plot a Robin Hood style robbery to right the wrong. Will they be caught? Can they overcome the forces arrayed against them? Will love and followship endure? A combined caper and morality tale, The Allotment Gang teaches us that you should not mess with gardeners!

About Steven Carter

Originally from Liverpool, but educated in Bromsgrove (South Bromsgrove High School) where his parents still live, Steven Carter died tragically early, in late 2023. A Historian and teacher with degrees from Manchester University, Steven was a Justice of the Peace and Labour Councillor in Macclesfield for many years. This book, with its locus in and around Bromsgrove, was his first novel. It explores themes, locations and characters that will be familiar to many in North Worcestershire, but are of broad appeal to those who like a good tale.

www.ingramcontent.com/pod-product-compliance
Lightning Source LLC
Chambersburg PA
CBHW020412210626
46816CB00006BB/2242